Books by

COLBY RODOWSKY

What About Me?

Evy-Ivy-Over

P.S. Write Soon

A Summer's Worth of Shame

The Gathering Room

H, My Name Is Henley

Keeping Time

Julie's Daughter

Fitchett's Folly

Sydney, Herself

Dog Days

Lucy Peale

Hannah In Between

Sydney, Invincible

Remembering Mog

Remembering Mog

Remembering Mog

COLBY RODOWSKY

Farrar Straus Giroux ✎ New York

Published in Canada by HarperCollins*CanadaLtd*
Printed in the United States of America
Designed by Filomena Tuosto
First edition, 1996
Second printing, 1996

Library of Congress Cataloging-in-Publication Data
Rodowsky, Colby F.
Remembering Mog / Colby Rodowsky. — 1st ed.
    p.   cm.
    [1. Murder—Fiction. 2. Death—Fiction. 3. Family life—Fiction.]
I. Title.
PZ7.R6185Re   1996   [Fic]—dc20   95-30616   CIP   AC

For Beverly Reingold and Margaret Ferguson

Remembering Mog

One

I saw it as soon as I turned the corner. The windows in Mog's room were open, the screens shoved up, the curtains, drawn outside by the breeze, flapping wildly.

She's home, I thought; she's home. And I started to run, sailing over the uneven sidewalk, along the path to the house, across the porch, through the front hall with its player piano, abandoned drum set, and pie safe bulging with hats and scarves and mismatched gloves, and on up the stairs.

I caught hold of the doorframe to Mog's room and stood there swaying.

"I'm cleaning," said Reilly.

"Oh, yes, I see," I said.

"Yes." Reilly's face clouded over and got a bruised look that let me know she'd seen me flying down the street; that she knew what I'd been thinking. The same way, when Mog and I were little, she'd always known when we needed a Band-Aid or a cup of chamomile tea. Reilly, Mary Ellen Reilly, only no one ever called her that, was a kind of grandmother-aunt combination who was actually my father's second cousin or first cousin once removed or something. She had moved in temporarily years ago, after her husband died, back when Grandma and Granddad Fitzhugh still lived in the house. And when Moma and Dad inherited the place, they got Reilly, too, along with the player piano, the drums, a collection of umbrella stands, and late cousin George's model airplanes that still hung from the living room ceiling.

"Yes," said Reilly, her voice yanking me back to the present. "I felt restless this afternoon and wanted to get into something, to clean something. And it's always easier to clean something that's already clean." She stopped and bit her lip for a minute before going on. "I mean, you know, the way Mog had everything so—what's the word . . ."

"Monastic," I said.

The phone rang and Reilly dropped her dustcloth and started out the door. "That might be the library. I called the Infocenter with a question—well, it was for the crossword puzzle, but a question is a question, right? And anyway, before she went out, your mother said to tell you she'd be back with the car before it's time for you to leave for Erin's." Her words trailed after her as she went into her room at the end of the hall.

I gathered up the pieces of the vacuum cleaner, dragged them off to the linen closet, shoved them inside, closed the door, and leaned on it for a minute to keep it from popping open. Then, instead of heading for my own room, I went back to Mog's, going over to the windows, pulling the curtains in, and lowering the screens. I turned and sat on the radiator cover.

"Monastic," I had said to Reilly. "Monastically simple," Mog had said to me the day she totally purged her room. "You all may want to live in the clutter capital of the world, but I'm going for the monastically simple," she'd said just before she sang out "Ta-dum" and threw the door open for us to see.

It was a Saturday in the spring of her senior year, that sort of deceptive, almost fake, spring where the air is warm and misty but there are still snow patches under the bushes and along the north side of the house. Reilly was doing her crossword puzzle at the kitchen table, and Moma was having a cup of tea and flipping through her file box, trying to find what she'd done at Amanda Jefferson's birthday party *last* year. Moma's the Party Person—capital "P"s and balloons on her business cards and in the ads she runs in the newspaper—specializing in putting on children's birthday parties. She has a bunch of themes, and since a lot of her clients use her year after year, she has to be careful not to do the same thing for the same kid again.

Our brother, Cricket, who was twelve at the time, had taken his lacrosse stick and headed out the door, and my father was talking about how it was a good day for cutting back the rose bushes.

Mog and I were going to the Funky Forties, this really cool secondhand clothing store in Mount Washington, and she'd even talked Dad into letting her use the car. She'd promised me that after we were finished shopping and had had lunch *and* stopped at the library to get the books for her history term paper, she'd take me out to Loch Raven and let me practice driving. Which was incredibly nice of her, because I was still only fifteen and not even close enough to sixteen to get my learner's permit, and if Moma and Dad had known they'd've totally freaked out. I mean, our parents are casual—but only about things that don't really matter, like the dog sleeping on the couch and popcorn for breakfast and spending the whole of a rainy Sunday watching Woody Allen movies instead of cleaning our rooms.

While Mog went to get dressed, I helped Moma load her stuff into the car. I was just coming back inside when Mog came down the stairs, holding a gross-looking orange-and-green blob at arm's length.

"Do you know what this is?" she screeched. "Just *look* at it."

I leaned closer, pretending to examine the object from all angles, though I knew full well what it was. "A green sweater with orange cat fur," I said finally.

"Exactly. *My* green sweater," said Mog. "With *Ben's* fur. And it's disgusting. Anyway, it was my favorite green sweater and I wanted to wear it today because it's almost spring and almost St. Patrick's Day, and when I went to get it out of the back of my closet I found that that animal had been sleeping there, maybe all winter. And it's lucky for him he didn't poop there."

"They don't poop where they sleep," I said.

"You just think it's funny, don't you? But what can I expect from someone who lets the *dog* sleep in her bed."

I started to tell her what a comforting feeling it was, whenever I woke in the night, to feel Homer's solid weight against my legs, but Mog was still going on, her long blond hair swinging with every shake of her head.

"Other people don't live like this—in hodgepodge heaven. Other people don't have heaps on top of piles on top of clutter. They don't live with the smells of dogs they've never known, from before their time, and with the presence of long-gone relatives. Millions of them."

"But, Moggie, we always *liked* that. We always said thank heavens we weren't stuck in some neat little house in suburbia."

"Well, *some* of us grow up," said Mog. "Some of us grow *out* of it."

"Dad didn't. And Reilly. And Moma—and it wasn't even her family. Besides," I hurried on, "we were always glad about the millions of relatives—their pictures and the way we could *feel* them, here, in the house. Same as we were glad about cousin George's airplanes in the living room and—"

"And every toy anybody ever owned stuffed up in the attic," said Mog.

"That's a play, *Toys in the Attic,* by Lillian Hellman. It was on our extra-credit reading list this year," I said.

"Go ahead, make light of it," said Mog.

Though I hadn't exactly been doing that, I didn't bother trying to explain.

"As of this minute," she went on, "I'm streamlining my life—starting with my room. And that means no Funky Forties, no lunch out, or anything else you might have had in mind for today." She dropped the hair-sweater and punt-kicked it at the door, stopping only long enough to nudge it out onto the back porch before she turned and went upstairs.

I did the breakfast dishes and wiped the counters and filled Homer's water bowl. I went out onto the porch and retrieved Mog's sweater, shaking it as hard as I could and watching Ben's orangy-red hair float off and hang suspended in the air. I spread the sweater on the railing, figuring I'd give it a few more shakes every time I passed that way, until it was defuzzed enough to go in the washer. Then I went inside, wandering through the first floor, thinking that maybe it was what Mog said it was: hodgepodge heaven. And that I liked it that way.

I stopped in front of the picture on the wall between the front windows in the living room. The Mizpah Picture, as we called it, was a painting on wood of two little girls, their faces turned and shadowed by sunbonnets. Underneath it were the words "The Lord Watch between Me and Thee, When We Are Absent One from Another." Which, according to Reilly, is what *Mizpah* means.

When Mog and I were little we always thought the picture was of us, and even after we were old enough to read the date—1886—and knew it wasn't, we still secretly believed it was. We loved the painting, and the sound of the words, and years ago we used to torment Cricket by telling him he couldn't really be part of the family if he wasn't in the picture.

I stood there for a minute, running the tip of my finger over the Mog figure, the Annie figure. After that I went up to my room and tried to think of what to do for the rest of the day.

Mostly what I did was listen to Mog and the sounds of moving and shoving and rearranging that came from her room. In between, I changed the sheets on my bed, took Homer for a walk, talked on the phone, and made a pan of lemon squares not from a mix. Every once in a while Mog would appear, dragging a chair, a dresser, a washstand into another room, and once, after lunch, she grabbed Cricket and had him help her carry her old oak

bedstead up to the attic. She left things in the hall outside her door, and when I was sure she was otherwise
occupied, I'd sneak out and sift through them, appro-
priating an old wire birdcage and the white wicker bed
tray she'd had in her room since she'd had the mumps
in fifth grade.

Late in the afternoon my father came in for a Coke,
and together we sat at the kitchen table in a splotch of
sunlight. "Mog's streamlining her life," I said. "She says
that we live in hodgepodge heaven, only some of us grow
out of it."

"Hmmmmm," said Dad, rubbing his fingers back and
forth across his chin so that his whiskers made a sandpa-
pery sound. "She may be right, but cut her some slack.
It's probably senior-year angst, Sturm und Drang, and
all that." He grinned, licked his index finger, and pretended to make two marks in the air. "Two with one
blow," he said.

I knew he was talking about clichés. It's part of the
family lore that Dad half-seriously thinks he could've
been a famous writer except that his high-school English
teacher permanently damaged his psyche by dubbing him
the Cliché King of 4B. Now he sells insurance instead.

We were still sitting there when Moma came in, dropping pieces of cake wrapped in birthday napkins on the
table and pulling up a chair.

"How was the party?" Dad asked.

"It was really good," she said. "I used a dance theme,
and instead of playing games we did improvisations, and
you should've *seen* those kids."

Then Mog appeared in the doorway, her sleeves rolled

up, her face smudged with dirt. And back to her regular self. "Okay, it's time for the great unveiling. Come on, you guys."

As we followed her up the stairs, she called back over her shoulder, "I hope you like it. I mean, you all may want to live in the clutter capital of the world, but right now I'm going for the monastically simple.

"Ta-dum," she said, sweeping her arms out and opening the door at the same time.

And I gasped and breathed in the clean lemon smell and said, "Oh, my. Oh, Mog."

I mean, we were talking Spartan here. Her mattress and box spring sat directly on the floor, which was bare and obviously just polished. Except for a poster of Picasso's *Woman in White,* the walls were naked, with only ghostly shadows to show where the pictures used to be. The bookcase had been plundered, and the books that were left stood straight and unyielding. And in the closet her shoes were lined in formation on the floor.

"I thought if it was okay, maybe we could go to Ikea and get one of those plain-looking dressers," said Mog, pointing out the socks and sweaters and underwear piled neatly on the shelves.

Back in the center of the room she spun slowly around before she stopped, clearly waiting. "Well?" she said.

"It's—something," said Dad.

"Indeed," said Moma.

"Amazing," I said. Which is one of those words that can go either way.

After a while the radiator cover felt hard, and I stood up and closed the windows. I moved over and sat on the end of the bed, smoothing the crinkly material of the spread with the flat of my hand and thinking how that day seemed so long ago, and as close as today.

The day my sister Mog was killed.

The day she was murdered.

Two

I'd had my shower and was dressed before Moma got home. In fact, I was dressed and undressed and re-dressed. I'd changed my top three times, added a scarf, a belt, and dangly earrings, and then gone back to what I'd had on the first time around. I'd pulled my hair behind my ears and let it fly loose and bunched it up, trying to see what it would look like if I cut it short. I'd used blush, rubbed it off, and used some more. I'd put on a floppy straw hat that hung from my bedpost, stood in front of the mirror for a bit, and decided to go with it.

It's not that I'm vain. Not obsessively, anyway. And I wasn't going with anybody—to the party or in general. I wasn't even *looking,* at least I don't think I was. It was just that I couldn't seem to stay still, I guess because of the thoughts that had been slam-banging around inside my head for the last few days, which all had to do with my best friend, Erin McNabb, having a graduation party for the senior class that night.

The same as her sister, Jenny, had had a party for *her* class—Mog's class—two years ago. The night Mog was . . . the night it happened.

And the weird thing was that I'd been talking to Mog about it all week, the way I did sometimes. About how it was like déjà vu, or a movie I'd already seen, a book I'd read. Only now, suddenly, and maybe for the first time, talking to Mog wasn't enough. I needed somebody to *answer* me.

I opened my door and stepped out into the hall, and the emptiness of the house almost swallowed me up. It was then that I remembered Reilly calling in to me while I was in the shower, saying that she was off to an early movie with a friend.

Cricket had come in from school and gone out again.

Dad wasn't home yet, and even if he had been, for the last two years he's had this shrunken look, as if he were backing away to a place where I couldn't follow.

As for Moma—all I can say about Moma now is that for a long time she's been pretty deeply into a game of Let's Pretend. And all you need to play is a lot of denial.

I thought, the way I had so many times before, that I hadn't lost only my sister when Mog died, but my mother and father as well.

I stood holding on to the banister, watching the sunlight through the stained-glass windows along the stair wall. For a crazy moment I even thought of calling Bobby Ritter, the boy who'd been with Mog that night, but the last time I ran into him around the neighborhood he'd looked sort of distracted, and from what I'd heard he was still having problems of his own, and it didn't seem fair to dump on him.

There was Erin, of course, except by this time she'd be running around doing last-minute stuff for the party. Besides, my friends had done enough: letting me talk, or not talk; cry, or not cry. Now they'd moved on to thoughts of graduation and summer jobs and college, the rest of their lives.

I had just started back into my room when Erin called, asking me to come out as soon as I could and to pick up a bag of ice on my way, and saying why didn't I plan to spend the night so I wouldn't have to drive home alone so late by myself. I said I would if Moma didn't need her car too early in the morning, and she said if that was the case, to call someone quickly for a ride and she'd bring me home after graduation practice tomorrow. I hung up and threw some clothes into a bag and had just gotten down to the kitchen when my mother came in.

"You all set?" she asked, taking a pitcher of iced tea out of the refrigerator and pouring herself a glass.

"Yes, just about," I said. "Except that Erin wants me to spend the night unless that's a problem with the car, and if it is I'm pretty sure I can get a ride."

The kitchen was quiet except for the sound of water dripping in the sink. My mother cut a lemon and squeezed a piece into her glass. She added sugar. I thought for a minute that her hand shook, but I wasn't sure.

"No problem," she said. "Your father and I are going to the Benton wedding tomorrow, so we'll use his car."

I wanted her to go on, to say something more. I wanted her to tell me that she'd rather I stayed home tonight, that she needed me here, that she remembered what had happened to Mog. Instead she picked up the mail and her glass of tea, carrying them over to the table.

I grabbed the keys and headed out and had just started up the street when I saw Cricket. He waved his arms and did his fake traffic-cop routine as he gestured me over to the curb, then came to stand by the driver's side, leaning in the open window.

"Yeah," he said. And then, after a long pause, "You okay?"

"I am now," I said, and then I kissed him, quickly and on the side of his face, which wasn't something I'd dared to do since he was really little. Because we're not a kissy family.

Cricket yelped and jumped back. "Dog germs—sister germs," he called as he darted up onto the curb and disappeared through the bushes.

I sat there for a minute, looking after him and feeling weirdly better.

"Great hat, Annie," said Mrs. McNabb when I'd knocked and stepped into the kitchen.

"You think so?" I asked, squinting at myself in the front of the microwave. "I couldn't decide."

"Yes, it's definitely you," she said, fitting aluminum foil over the top of this fantastic seven-layer Mexican dip she makes and sliding it into the refrigerator. "Erin's in the shower, maybe getting dressed by now, so you can run on up. Or, if you don't mind, you might check around outside first and see if we've forgotten anything."

I went through the house, stopping in the dining room to look at the buffet table, covered with a red-and-white-checked cloth and piled with plates and serving dishes, and with knives and forks rolled in paper napkins and tied with ribbons. From there I went out the front door and along the drive. Erin lives in what is sort of the country, where there are no sidewalks or streetlights and the houses are far apart, plus at the side of their property there's someone else's empty field, which gives the feeling of endless space. The way I look at it, it's an okay place to visit—but I wouldn't want to live there. Just as *she* wouldn't want to live where *I* do.

I went past the tables set up on the lawn and down toward the swimming pool.

"Hey, Annie, I like your hat," called Erin's sister, Jenny, as she surfaced in the deep end and swam to the side. "Where'd you get it?"

"Off my bedpost," I answered. "It's been there for ages and I just thought, Why not?"

Jenny climbed out of the pool and reached for a towel. "How about those lights?" she said, pointing at the Japanese lanterns strung through the trees overhead. "It took Erin and me forever to get them up there, and when we were done my father got home and decided that the wires were an accident waiting to happen and he's out now getting another extension cord. Anyway, I'll see you later. Somebody's picking me up in fifteen minutes and I've got to get ready."

Jenny headed inside, and I went over to sit on the swing hanging from a giant elm tree. I pushed off as hard as I could, picking up my feet and swooping forward. I felt my hat being lifted up and carried away, and I turned in time to see it land in a patch of clover. I pumped my legs, sailing higher and higher, leaning back and watching the branches overhead. After a while I let the swing slow on its own, and when it stopped I sat there, my head against the rope.

I looked at the sheet, strung like a banner between two trees, with the words CONGRATULATIONS, SENIORS painted on it, and I thought how Mog might have sat in this very place two years ago and seen it, too. Just as she must have seen the lanterns in the trees, the tables on the lawn, the buffet table with the red-and-white-checked cloth. And, like a sudden fog moving in, that other night crowded around me.

It had been hot the Friday before graduation, the night of Jenny McNabb's party. Mog was taking Bobby Ritter, her sometimes boyfriend and a really great guy whose only problem was that he liked Mog more than she liked him. This wasn't all bad from my standpoint, though, because a lot of times Mog would let me go along with the two of them—to the movies or to get pizza, and once even to Ocean City for the day. I didn't see why tonight should be any different, but when I asked her if she and Bobby would give me a ride to Erin's when they went to the party, and bring me home again, she got this all-over serious look on her face and shook her head and said, "I'm sorry, Annie, but not tonight. We just can't."

"How come?" I said. "There's nothing to do here and Erin wants me to come out. She says they have a ton of really great food, and we can go swimming, and besides, we want to check out the seniors, see what you all do."

"Spend the night, then. Erin won't care. We can take you out. It's just coming home we can't manage."

"I *can't*. I have to baby-sit first thing in the morning, and there's no way Moma's going to come out there and get me that early. Anyway, why not? Bring me home, I mean. It's not as if you two have the romance of the century going."

"That's the point," said Mog. "What I have to tell him. And don't try to talk me out of it."

"Out of what?"

"Telling Bobby."

"Telling Bobby what?"

"That there's no chemistry between us, no spark. And how we can never be anything but friends and he should stop wasting his time and put himself back in circulation. How there are a ton of girls out there for him and he'd better do something about meeting them. That's what."

"Oh, Mog," I said. "You can't. Not right before graduation. Not to Bobby. He's so nice. So right—"

"So not for me," said Mog. "Besides, I've rehearsed it, practiced exactly what I'm going to say—and I'm going to say it tonight, on the way home from the party. And don't start with the guilt trip. I know what I'm doing."

I turned away from her, swallowing hard at the sudden rush of tears. "He'll be better off without you," I said as I went out of the room.

"That's what I've been trying to tell you," Mog called after me.

I slammed my door.

I stayed upstairs when Bobby came to pick up Mog for the party, in case I cried when I saw him. Then Moma, Dad, Reilly, Cricket, and I had supper on the back porch, and I studied for my French exam even though it was Friday. Later I talked to Erin on the phone for ages, while she gave me a play-by-play of the party and who wore what and who came with whom and how Delia Crowell's date stashed a cooler of beer under a hydrangea bush and Erin's father caught him and sent him packing (and Delia with him)—but without the beer—and how Jenny said she was humiliated and could never show her face in school again and how Mr. McNabb said it was good that school was over for the seniors and that the only thing left was practice tomorrow and graduation on Sunday.

After that I sat on the porch for a while and smelled the honeysuckle and the cat pee in the bushes. It was just past eleven when I went upstairs to get ready for bed, feeling sort of happy and sad, as though I were playing a part in a play (maybe Frankie in *The Member of the Wedding*) and watching myself from the outside in. As I brushed my teeth I thought about what a perfect night it was—for everyone except Bobby Ritter, who maybe at that very moment was hearing words he didn't want to hear. I was still angry with Mog for saying them, and for not liking Bobby as much as I wanted her to, though I really sort of admired her for telling him the truth, even though she knew it was going to hurt.

Grabbing a piece of paper and a purple Magic Marker, I wrote, "What'd he say? Was he brokenhearted?" and took it in and propped it on her pillow. Then I went back in my room and got into bed, hoping that when she came in she'd wake me and tell me all about it.

"Where's this hat everybody's been talking about?" said Erin, coming across the lawn toward me. I blinked a minute, unfolded myself from the swing, and went to get it.

"What d'you think?" I said, putting it on and modeling it for her.

"Great—I wish I'd thought of it," said Erin.

"Right, and if the party gets dull, we can use it for a Frisbee," I said as we walked back to the house.

Three

The party wasn't dull, though. Everybody in the senior class came, which meant there were fifty of us, because St. Christopher's—except we call it St. Kit's—where we all go, is this small, private girls' school where Reilly actually went when *she* was young and where there's even a picture of her in some bloomery gym suit in an upstairs hall. Most people brought a date, and Erin had invited a bunch of extra guys, including Hank Donellan, whom I probably would've asked if I'd gotten around to asking anyone. And because even though Baltimore's a city it's a lot like a small town, too, we pretty much knew one another.

We ate supper when it was just beginning to get dark, with the lanterns shining in the trees and citronella candles on the tables. For dessert there was a giant sheet cake with "Way to Go, Seniors" in red letters and rolled-up diplomas made of icing on the corners. Then, later on, Mrs. McNabb brought out six-foot subs with the works, in case we got hungry again, which we did. There were coolers filled with sodas and iced tea and juice, but that was all. And the weird thing was that except for a couple of guys who left early, I don't think anybody really cared. Partly because Erin had *totally* warned us what would happen if anybody tried to sneak alcohol in, but mostly, I think, because at school we'd had speakers from both MADD and SADD—and the stories they'd told had given us cold chills.

We danced, and even sang some, and played volleyball. (My hat was long gone.) A crowd went swimming, swearing that it wasn't cold but dashing for the house and dry clothes as soon as they got out of the water. And in between, in the little lulls in the evening, I pinched myself and told myself that this was now. Now, now, now.

Mr. McNabb wandered around all night with a video camera, asking the seniors to say something for posterity, which was pretty weird, but we did it anyway. About eleven o'clock Sister Leonard, the headmistress of St. Kit's, arrived with Frank Rigby and Ellen Margolis, the homeroom teachers. Then someone suggested that we sing the school song—which was *definitely* weird, but we did that, too. Afterward things started to mellow out. A few couples disappeared into the shadows, but most of us just sat around talking about how, except for practice tomorrow and graduation on Sunday, this would probably be the last time we were all together. Until we got old and went to alumnae meetings.

When the party was over, Erin and her mother and father and I cleaned up. And then, after her parents went to bed and because we weren't sleepy, we went into the family room and watched the video Mr. McNabb had made. A lot of what people said was pretty predictable—about the years in high school being so great and feeling sad to leave and keeping in touch—so mostly what we did was mentally try to *age* everyone, to see what they'd look like in ten, twenty, thirty years.

"The same, only older. And still different from each other," I said as we waited for the tape to rewind.

"Except us," said Erin. "We'll stay the same without getting older, right?"

"Right."

As we headed up the stairs, I thought how one of the things I liked best about St. Kit's was that it wasn't one of those cookie-cutter schools where the kids are all alike. I mean, we're sort of a mixture, coming, the way we do, from a bunch of backgrounds and living in neighborhoods all over town. And some are rich (Erin) and some aren't (most of the rest of us); some are on scholarship, some not. And basically it had never mattered.

After Erin went to sleep, I lay there looking at the shapes of things in the moonlight: doors and windows, even the computer monitor. I rolled onto my side, my stomach, my back again. I played games—A, my name is Alice, My husband's name is Alan, I come from Alabama, and I eat apples—hoping the singsongy rhythm would put me to sleep. I went through the alphabet twice and was still wide awake. What seemed like ages later, I got up and tiptoed down the stairs, easing the kitchen door open and going outside to the patio. I curled up in a redwood rocker, drawing my T-shirt around my legs.

"That's better," I said, letting my breath out in a swoosh, and for a while I sat listening to the sound of silence. Then suddenly the thoughts that had been hovering just off to the side caught up with me and circled around me like so many demons. "That night, that night," they taunted. "That night again."

The quiet was broken. The trees stirred overhead, the gate to the pool creaked. There was a rustling in the bushes, and I pressed my face into my knees. But not seeing was worse and I stood up, turned my chair, and sat down again, staring at the shadows that seemed to twist and dance across the lawn. I pushed back at the thoughts crowding against me—thoughts of how the person who had done that to Mog was still out there, how he'd never been caught, how, even though the police described it as a random crime, and how I knew it didn't make any real sense to think he'd come after Cricket or Reilly or Moma or Dad, or even me, it was still a possibility. That he could do again what he had done before.

I fought until I couldn't fight anymore, and then I jumped up, toppling the chair, and ran inside, bumping into Mrs. McNabb just as she was opening the door.

"Annie?" she said, catching me by the shoulders. "I thought I heard someone go outside." She held me at arm's length, looking at me for a minute, then led me into the family room, to the end of the couch, where she bundled me in an afghan. "Are you all right?"

"Y-yes." I swallowed hard. "I'm fine."

"This has got to be a bad time for you," she said, sitting beside me and curling the edge of the afghan between her fingers. "And I'm not at all sure we should have had this party. Maybe it was too much of a reminder. Too—"

"No," I broke in. "The party was great and I *wanted* to be here. It's just that sometimes . . ." I shook my head at the words that wouldn't come.

We sat without saying anything until Mrs. McNabb got up and went into the kitchen, where I heard her opening and closing the refrigerator, heard the beep of the microwave.

"Here's some cocoa for you," she said, coming back. "Maybe it'll help you sleep."

I reached for it, wrapping my fingers around the mug and letting the warmth seep into me. "Thank you," I said when I had finished.

"Well," she said after a while, "I'm going on up. Do you want to go back to bed or . . ."

"I'd rather stay here for a bit if it's okay. But I'll be along soon."

She started to leave, then turned and sat down again. "Look, Annie, this is something I've been wanting to say to you, except that I didn't—I don't want to butt in." She reached into the pocket of her robe and took out a small white card, holding it for a minute before she handed it over to me. "It's just that I've seen you hurting for a long time now, and this is the name of someone I know of—a counselor—who might be able to help if you ever felt like talking to her. Just hang on to it, in case you need it." And she gave me a quick kiss and headed for the stairs.

After she had gone I sat holding the card, rubbing my fingers against it as the clock struck four.

It had been four o'clock when the police came that night. I had awakened to the sounds of the doorbell ringing and Homer's barking and gone out into the hall. The lights were on downstairs, and I could see my father, just reaching for the doorknob, with Moma standing in back of him and clasping her dragon kimono across her chest. There was a rumble of voices as two policemen stepped into the house. And right away I knew that something terrible had happened.

Somehow Reilly and I got down the steps and moved in close to my parents in time to hear Moma asking the officers if they wanted an iced tea, or maybe a Coke, talking about the weather being hot for June and a bunch of other stuff as if they were neighbors come for a visit, as if it were four in the *afternoon*. To keep them from saying what they'd come to say.

Which was—

Which was that—

Even now, all this time later, I have trouble saying it. Which was that Moggie was dead. That Bobby was hurt. And my mother went on as if she'd heard only part of what they were saying and that part didn't have anything to do with us. She talked about accidents and traffic and the roads in the county. About alcohol—but she knew that wasn't the case with Bobby Ritter, because he was a splendid boy and the kind you'd want your daughter to go out with.

"Do either of you gentlemen have a daughter?" she asked, looking from one to the other. And without waiting for them to answer she said, "Anyway, we've talked to the children about drinking and driving and how they could always call home for a ride, no matter what time."

Her voice was shrill. My father tried to stop her, saying, "Clara, Clara, the detectives are trying to tell us something." But she started in again about iced tea and its being hot for June. She ran over and undid the safety locks on the window nearest the couch and pushed it up.

That was when Reilly went to her and took her by the

shoulders and sat her down on the green chair heaped high with cushions and said, "Listen." And overhead cousin George's model airplanes swung slowly in the draft from the window.

Dad, Reilly, and I moved over to the couch, except that after a minute my father got up and went to sit on the arm of Moma's chair, his hand on her shoulder. The policemen sat down and the older one, with the sort of potbelly, who said his name was Leggett and seemed to be in charge, spoke. He said that Mog was dead, that Bobby had been wounded, and it was pretty obvious from the way he edged around his words that he wasn't talking about fog and winding country roads and traffic accidents.

Then his words turned into a jumble and I'm still not able to reach back and sort them all out. ". . . shot . . . your daughter has been shot . . . killed . . . dead . . ." At one point the word *murder* surfaced and drifted out into the room. Who said it? My father? My mother? Reilly? Me? Detective Leggett said, "Homicide," and I remember wondering if by changing the word he hoped to make it less real, less stark.

"How?"

"Where?"

"But why?"

We asked our questions like bit players acting out our parts.

It had happened in Fells Point, a part of town down on the waterfront that is mostly old but sort of trendy now.

"No," said my mother, looking from one to the other, her eyes wide. "No. She wasn't *in* Fells Point, Mog wasn't. Jenny McNabb was having a party and she lives way out in the county, near Sparks. It was a graduation party. Graduation is Sunday afternoon at four o'clock. It's always on a Sunday at St. Kit's, and practice is tomorrow—today—this afternoon. I hope those girls aren't going to be too tired, but they're young, they bounce back."

For a minute Moma looked puzzled and shook her head, but before anyone could say anything she went on—about Jenny's party and what Mog had worn and how maybe some of the seniors would get together for lunch before practice today.

Detective Leggett looked at my father as if waiting for him to do something. Then he got up, reaching for a small straight chair. He took it over and put it down in front of my mother, sitting on it.

"That really isn't very sturdy," she said, laughing a thin, fluty laugh. "Years ago a friend who used to be a football player—or maybe he was a wrestler—came to a party and picked that chair out of all the chairs in the house and sat on it and it crumbled under him and it took every bit of magic by that wonderful old furniture company down on Maryland Avenue to put it right again."

Detective Leggett ignored her and began to speak, and his words, though careful and deliberate, gathered momentum like a barrel rolling down a hill. "Your daughter Mog has been shot, has been killed, and the young man, Bobby Ritter, has been wounded. We were able to piece together what must have happened because Bobby regained consciousness shortly after we got there and we talked to him before they took him away in the ambulance.

"Apparently, the two of them left the party around

twelve, but instead of coming home they took the expressway into downtown Baltimore and then over to Fells Point, where they parked on Ann Street and walked down by the water." He broke off and hit his fist against the palm of his other hand. "It's not safe out there. These kids have got to learn they'd be better off on their own back porch, or making out in somebody's basement."

I jerked forward in my seat. But it wasn't like that, I wanted to scream, because Mog wanted to *talk* to him— to tell him—

But when the detective asked me if I had anything to say, I shook my head and waited for him to go on.

"Bobby wasn't clear about how long they'd stayed down at the water, but they got back just in time to interrupt someone breaking into the car. Bobby yelled and grabbed for Mog, but she pulled away from him. He's a little muddled here, but he thinks he remembers her running *at* the car, at the shooter himself. There were shots and your daughter fell. The Ritter boy was hit and threw himself forward, landing on top of her, trying to get her to speak. But she couldn't—she—we think she died instantly."

"How was she hurt?" my father asked, so softly that we had to strain to hear him.

The policeman stood up and moved his chair back, as if he wanted to distance himself from what was coming next. "Your daughter was shot twice in the head and once in the chest," he said. "And another bullet shattered the boy's arm and he lost a lot of blood, though the expectation is that he'll be okay."

There was a long silence in the room. Homer sighed in

his sleep and inched closer to my foot, and after what seemed like hours my father said, "Who?" Just the one word, but I think we all knew what he meant was "Who did this? Who did this to Mog?"

"We don't know, Mr. Fitzhugh. But we're onto it already. The crime lab's going over the car, we'll check the neighborhood, and there's one witness so far—a woman on Ann Street who heard the shots, looked out her window in time to see someone ducking into an alley, and called 911. Sometimes these guys—the ones who pull this kind of thing—they're not too smart. Sometimes they screw up big time. But we'll keep you informed."

After Detective Leggett stopped talking, the silence settled over us again. We sat like statues, and I thought maybe we'd stay that way forever, that we'd never move out from under the terrible weight that had come down on top of us. I looked at my parents' faces, and it's hard to say which was worse: my mother's, which seemed to have been wiped clean, or my father's, which showed that he'd taken in every word the policeman had said.

Reilly sat with her head back, staring at the ceiling. After a while she got up and went over to close the window Moma had opened, as if sealing us off from the world outside.

The other policeman, the younger one with the frizzy hair whose name was Carter, said, "We're going to need someone to come with us and identify the body."

My father got up slowly. "Just let me go upstairs and put some clothes on," he said.

When he came down he went to my mother, speaking softly and telling her that he had to go with the officers, that he'd hurry back. Then he put his arm around my shoulders and walked me to the door. "Take care of her," he said.

I watched him go along the walk and get into the police car. The sky over the housetops was streaked with light, and I stood there for a few minutes watching Mr. Clemens from across the street help his old dog down the porch steps and onto the grass.

When I got back inside, Moma was sitting just the way I'd left her, only Reilly had moved closer and was holding her hand. "I'll make some tea," I said, heading for the kitchen. But as I stood waiting for the water to boil, my mother came in all in a rush. She rummaged in the top of the cupboard for the coffee maker we never used. She rooted in a drawer for filters and reached for the canister, scooping, measuring.

"But—none of us drinks coffee," I said.

She wiped spilled grounds off the counter and ran water into the pot, pouring it through the opening in the top of the machine, moving like a windup toy gone haywire.

I stood in front of her, blocking her way. "Moma, listen. Something's happened to Mog. The police were here and they tried to tell you and Dad's gone down to—"

"I know," she said, reaching in back of me to push the plug into the wall.

The water dripped down and the smell of coffee filled the air and hung there as Moma, Reilly, and I sat at the table and drank tea. The kitchen grew brighter, with sunlight filling the corners and catching on the wooden animals marching along the windowsill, the bowls and pitchers and jumble of cookbooks.

Reilly turned off the light just as we heard the clock radio come on in my parents' bedroom upstairs. The announcer's voice was muffled, his words unclear.

Just then I remembered that Cricket had spent the night with a friend up the street. "Cricket!" I said, jumping up. "He's at Roger's and we have to get to him before—I mean, there could be something on the radio—he should be here anyway." I started away from the table, but Moma caught my arm, holding it so that it hurt and then turned numb, pulling me back. Without saying anything, Reilly went upstairs, and in a few minutes I heard her going out the front door.

It seemed like ages before she and Cricket got back, and when they did I could tell, from the way his eyes seemed to burn in their sockets, that she had told him. He came into the room and headed straight for Moma, then veered suddenly, as if invisible rays were turning him away. Instead he moved over to the bench, to sit next to me. For a few minutes he tried to keep it all together and then, sort of choking and sputtering, he doubled over. I wrapped my arms around him and held him tight and tried to stop him from shaking. And more than anything I wanted someone to hold me the way I was holding him.

I shuddered and looked down to see that I was clutching a sofa cushion, rocking it from side to side. That Cricket was gone, and that other night along with him. I pushed the cushion away and stood up, balancing for a minute on legs that felt wobbly and not used to walking, before I headed out into the hall and back to Erin's room.

Four

The memories tagged along behind me, though, following me up the stairs and into Erin's room, crowding around me as I slipped into the bed under the window. At first I tried to ignore them, turning to the wall and thinking about tomorrow and the whole long summer stretching in front of me. But the harder I fought them, the harder they fought back, until finally I bunched the pillows against the headboard, settling there and letting the rest of that day sweep over me.

I had still been sitting at the table, holding Cricket, when the phone rang. Reilly answered it, and I could hear Mrs. Gibson's voice squawking from across the room, so I eased myself away from Cricket and went to take it.

"What happened to you, Annie?" Mrs. Gibson said before I'd barely had a chance to say hello. "I was expecting you to baby-sit twenty minutes ago. I *told* you we had to leave early. That's why we asked you and not someone else—because you're *reliable*. We're set to walk out the door as soon as you—"

"Mrs. Gibson, I can't—"

"Of *course* you can. You *must*. You *promised*."

"Something's happened," I said. And I hung up the phone.

For a while Mrs. Gibson's words seemed to hang suspended in the kitchen, drifting just overhead, until Reilly stirred, reaching for our mugs and setting them in the sink. "Come on, now," she said. "People will be stopping by, and we have to get ready. Showered and dressed."

My mother stood up like an obedient child, but when I tried to take her arm she shook me off and headed for the back stairs. I followed her, waiting in the upstairs hall for a minute, thinking that she would say something. Instead she went into her room and shut the door, without once looking over her shoulder.

When I'd had my shower and put on my clothes, I went to stand by the window, brushing my hair and looking out at the backyard. Cricket and Roger Carmody were sitting on the picnic table, their feet on one of the benches, lacrosse sticks on the grass. They didn't speak, and except that every once in a while Roger threw a ball up into the air and caught it, they hardly moved. But just seeing them there together like that gave me such a wallop of loneliness that I backed away from the window and sat down.

I was still sitting there when my father knocked on the door and came in. He stood for a minute fingering the light switch and shaking his head, I guess to keep me from asking anything, before he said, "I've talked to the funeral director, Annie, and they're going to need some clothes for your sister . . . to be, you know . . . and I can't ask your mother. If you could just . . ."

"I'll get them," I said, and kept on sitting there.

Dad shuffled his feet and jiggled the doorknob. "I'm heading on down there soon. To see to things. To make the arrangements. So whenever you can . . ." He dug in his pocket and pulled out a scrap of paper, handing it to me. "Here's a list of what they need."

"Now?" I said, but when I looked up he was gone.

I went into Mog's room and closed the door, but all of a sudden I felt trapped and opened it again. I looked at the list: underwear, hose, *no shoes*, jewelry, dress. The words *no shoes* seemed to lift off the paper, and I thought back to the time Granddad Fitzhugh died, when Mog was seven and I was five, and how the only thing we wanted to know was if he had his shoes on in the coffin. "No shoes," I whispered as I picked a Gap bag off the bed and rooted in the top drawer for underpants, a bra and half slip, a pair of panty hose. I tried to make my mind go blank, not to think of what I was doing as I took out the earring box and sorted through it for the silver hoops. My hands shook and earrings spilled onto the floor, clicking against the bare wood. I picked them up, hurrying and at the same time looking over my shoulder, for fear that Mog would catch me there, going through her stuff.

I pushed that thought away and went to the closet for her blue dress, stopping to check the hook on the inside of the door for her silver chain. It wasn't there. I went back to the dresser, looking in the jewelry box, sifting through drawers, feeling under sweaters, T-shirts, socks, until I remembered that Mog had been wearing it when she'd gone to Jenny's party. I turned around and saw the note I'd left propped on her pillow the night before, and right away I wanted to get out of there. I shoved the clothes into the bag, grabbed for the note, and ran.

My father was having a cup of tea at the kitchen table and I sat with him, waiting until he was finished before I gave him the bag of clothes. He sighed and got up and was reaching for his keys when my mother came in.

"I'm going with you," she said.

"You sure?" he asked.

"I'm sure."

Almost as soon as my parents left, the phone began to ring and neighbors started coming to the door, as if jungle drums had sent a message to the world. Someone brought a ham, someone else a casserole, a loaf of banana bread. Twice I went to call Erin, and twice I hung up without dialing. And then, a little while later, when I was trying to fit a pan of rice pudding into the refrigerator, she came in the back door.

"My mom dropped me off and she'll pick me up later," she said, handing me a goldfish in a bowl. For a minute I watched that crazy fish going round and round. Then I started to cry.

"Hey," said Erin, "quit slobbering on the fish." She took the bowl and put it on the counter, turning back and hanging on to me, letting me hang on to her.

My mother and father came home, and from the moment they walked in the door Moma seemed coated in plastic. She smiled, she talked, she greeted friends, but I could tell that she was somehow removed from what had happened. People reached for her, and she gave them fake air kisses and slipped away.

Mog's two best friends, Allison and Brooke, arrived

and left for graduation practice and came back again. Or maybe someone else did. I wasn't sure. A reporter came to the front door, and at first I thought he was somebody we knew and asked him in, and it wasn't till I saw the microphone and heard him ask, "How did it feel to learn your sister had been killed?" that I realized who he was. I was just standing there, not knowing how to get rid of him, when Reilly came along, her eyes blazing.

"Leave her alone," Reilly said, her voice both sharp and steely soft. "Leave us all alone." She had a broom in her hand and, as though he were trash, seemed to sweep him out, letting the screen slam shut after him and closing the big door and locking it, even though the sun was beating down and the house was stuffy from all the people crowded inside and no one had thought to open the downstairs windows since early that morning.

Somebody put lunch on the table and we sat down to eat—except for Moma, who just kept doctoring her iced tea with sugar and lemon and stirring it with a long-handled spoon until the ice melted and didn't click against the glass anymore. Another ham appeared, an angel food cake, and brownies. After that the time inched along, with us all mostly sitting around, not sure what we *should* be doing.

Erin's mother came to pick her up and stopped in for a while, holding me tight, and Cricket, too, and getting one of those air kisses from Moma. Father Nichols from our church arrived, carrying a fat music book, and he and Dad disappeared into the study. I tagged along, because I knew how Mog hated hymny-sounding hymns.

"The one about eagle's wings," I said when Father Nichols asked me if I had any suggestions. "And another one, it's Quaker, I think, and Mog really liked it and brought the program home from church one day so she could learn it, called 'How Can I Keep from Singing?' "

Dad took off his glasses and rubbed his eyes. "It's a funeral, Annie," he said.

"Yes, but it's Mog's," I said. And Father Nichols nodded his head.

Erin called almost as soon as she got home to tell me that Jenny said the entire senior class sort of fell apart at graduation practice, and that Sister Leonard had gotten a psychologist to come in and talk to the girls about what had happened to Mog, and that they'd all cried and hugged one another and said how they felt and then they'd hugged some more. And in a weird kind of way I wished I'd been there. She also said that Jenny said that Willa Reed said everyone should get a black band and wear it around the sleeve of her white graduation dress. That she'd seen it in a movie once. And that Allison had nearly freaked out and said that that was gross, and Mog would've hated it. Then Brooke suggested that they each pick a rose from their bouquets and bunch them all together and take them to the funeral home. *And* that Sister Leonard had stood up, her face crinkling into a sort of cat face, the way it does sometimes, and said, "That's a splendid solution, seniors, a splendid solution."

When Erin told me that, in a splattering of "s"s, I laughed out loud and wanted to tell it to Mog. That's when the hurting-all-over feeling settled down on me again.

I must have fallen asleep toward morning, because the next thing I knew, the room was bright with sunlight and

Erin was sitting on the bottom of my bed, bouncing up and down.

"I hate to wake you, but it's after eleven and we've got to get going. We can either eat something here or meet the others at Chili's before we go to practice. It's up to you."

"Chili's," I said, blinking and rolling out of bed, heading for the shower.

We were late getting to lunch, and Rachel and Chris and Nancy squished over and made room for us at their table. Afterward we went to school, to practice, which was pretty boring. Besides, since graduation at St. Kit's is held outside, under the trees, and is supposed to be sort of unstudied and spontaneous-looking, it felt like cheating to keep rehearsing it. But that was exactly what we did. Over and over and over again. And *then* we had to go inside and practice in the Assembly Hall, in case of rain, which would be pretty much a disaster because the hall isn't all that big *and* it has the acoustics of a locker room.

All that practicing gave me lots of time to think: about how, before, I'd pretty much followed after Mog, doing what she had done, only two years later, but *now*, with graduation and all, I would be stepping out ahead, going where she would never be able to go. And I was scared, the way I was scared the first time I climbed up to the high dive and stood looking down at the pool below. So scared that when Sister Leonard was lining us up for the last time and patted me on the shoulder on her way by, I thought about running after her, telling her that I couldn't go to graduation. That she'd have to send my diploma in the mail.

I didn't, though.

But instead of going home after practice, and almost without thinking about it, I found myself driving into downtown, heading over toward Fells Point. I parked on Thames Street and walked up to Ann, where I'd never actually been before, although I knew it as well as if I'd lived there. Because Mog had died there.

I stared up at the windows overhead, wondering where the witness had come to stand when she heard the shots and looked out to see Mog's killer, with the bald spot on top of his head (so that now every man with a bald spot was suspect, even bent old men) and the dark-colored sweatshirt. Worthless clues, as it turned out. I thought of going along, knocking on doors, but knew from what Detective Leggett had said that the woman had moved right after it happened. I wandered around, examining the ground for broken glass, as if nothing had changed. I wondered if the police had outlined Mog's body with chalk, the way they do on the TV, and peered down at the street, trying to make the lines reappear.

All around me people were walking by, unaware, and I wanted to catch hold of them and tell them that my sister had been killed on this spot, that Bobby Ritter had been savaged and, from what I'd heard, hadn't been right since. That none of us had. I went into a grocery store, blinking at the sudden darkness, and asked the proprietor if he remembered a murder two years ago.

"This is a safe neighborhood, girlie," he said. "A good neighborhood. Better'n some, better'n most. Ask anybody around here."

I backed out of the store and stood looking up and

down the street. Then I went over to Thames Street again, to the little plaza in front of the market, and sat on a bench, watching a pigeon and trying not to think. Until it was time to start for home.

Five

Nana and Popoo, who are Moma's parents, were there when I got home, sitting on the porch, drinking iced tea.

"Here's the graduate," called Nana as she patted the empty space next to her on the swing.

I kissed them both and sat down, saying, "It's good to see you guys. What time'd you get in? Are you staying here?" But I knew, even as I said it, that they weren't, that they always stayed at the inn over at Cross Keys because, as they put it, they liked to come and go as they pleased.

"To the house, around four-thirty; to town, around two. We stopped over at the hotel to settle in. You know your grandfather and I are hotel junkies. Besides, we like to be able to come and go as we please."

"I *knew* you'd say that," I said, pushing against the floor with my foot and sending the swing backward.

"Predictable, aren't we?" said Popoo.

"Yeah, but don't sweat it. It's okay. Remember the times you got an extra room for Mog and me and we stayed there with you and you let us order from room service late at night and use up all the postcards in the desk writing to our friends? Cricket got to go by himself when it was his turn, but I always thought Mog 'n' I had more fun. That us going together was somehow *better*. That it was—" And I stopped, suddenly not able to go on.

"Well, yes," said Popoo, sort of jumping into the silence. "Oh, and by the way, we brought a couple of cans of those peanuts today, the ones you like so well."

"And a ham," said Nana. "We brought a Smithfield ham, too. I thought your mother could use it tomorrow night, after the graduation, if she was having people in, only now she tells me—"

"That we're going out, *really* out, to the Milton Inn. It'll be you all and us and Reilly and Sue and Mike, because they're my godparents."

"That sounds very nice. And a lot less work for your mother."

"Yeah," I said. "Anyway, we're not much for having company anymore."

Nana reached over and squeezed my hand, and for a minute it looked as if she had something on her mind and wasn't sure whether to say it or not. Instead she sighed and did a kind of U-turn with her conversation, starting in on the news from home: that there was a new bakery in town, and Miss Lou, from next door, had had a fall, how the daffodils had been spectacular this year.

We *never* have company anymore, I thought. Haven't really since that other time, as if maybe we'd used up our allotment. Maybe had enough for a lifetime.

My grandparents had come then, too, the Saturday that Mog died, and I remember how Cricket and I had sat for ages on the porch swing with Popoo, one of his arms around each of us, while Nana stayed inside with my mother and father. And how, afterward, the three of us went for a walk around the block, not really saying much, but somehow it helped.

The cousins were there when we got back: Cindy, Tommy, Joan, Clark, and Mary. Along with their parents, my aunts and uncles. And they, the kids, were quieter than I ever remembered them being, hanging back or sticking to their mothers and fathers as if they were fastened there by Velcro. Even Tommy and Clark, who usually tease the cat or chase after Homer, or each other, up the back stairs and down the front, through the rooms on the first floor, and up the stairs again.

"They're waiting for Mog," whispered Reilly, coming to sit beside me and leaning close. And I knew she was right. Mog, the oldest of all the cousins, had always been the one who organized the rest, leading games of leapfrog or run, sheep, run, heading expeditions to the attic or the cellar, or junk-walking through the neighborhood, where she made a big deal over each found feather, each bit of polished stone. I looked across at Mary, her eyes dark and shadowed as she stared out into the hall, watching the stairs. I saw the way Joan twisted her fingers and heard her knuckles crack.

"Come on, you all," I said, getting up. "Let's go in the back room and play Monopoly."

"Naaah," said Mary. "Clark's too little. He'll wreck it."

"He can be *my* partner," said Reilly. "There are so many of us, we'll need to team up anyway."

The game didn't go well. I mean, nobody really *cared*

about getting doubles or passing GO or putting up hotels. Even Cricket, who was a Monopoly freak and a real entrepreneur, passed up opportunities to buy property and pretty much looked as if he'd rather be someplace else. But it was better than just sitting there and waiting for something that wasn't going to happen, for someone who wasn't going to come.

Reilly had just put a house on Park Place when Clark swept his arms across the board, sending houses and hotels, cards, markers, and stacks of money flying every which way.

"Mog's dead!" he shouted, his face turning purplish red. "She's dead—dead—"

"Shut up, Clark," said Mary, catching him by the arm. "You're not supposed to say that. Mom said not to. And *now* look what you've done—you've got to clean this *all* up."

It was as though we were caught inside a balloon that was ready to pop. I looked at Cricket, staring hard at the top of his tennis shoe, and at Clark, his face scrunched tight, then at Mary and Joan, Tommy and Cindy, all frozen around the table. I looked at Reilly, saw her nod slightly. I took a deep breath, fighting against the words as I said, "It's okay, Clark. We can't *not* talk about it. I mean what you said is true. Mog is dead."

But I didn't really believe it. Not then or later that night after everyone had left and it was just Moma, Dad, Cricket, Reilly, and me standing in the hall, or even the next morning when I pushed open the door to her room and saw that Mog's bed hadn't been slept in. I didn't believe it when we went to the funeral home and a smarmy-looking guy in a black suit showed us into a parlor that reeked of flowers, where a fake Mog in a blue dress and silver hoop earrings was lying in a coffin.

They've got it wrong, I thought. Mog wouldn't be lying there like that, all stiff and straight with a rosary in her hands, letting people stare at her. And the thoughts started to tangle in my head: If this wasn't Mog, then who was it? Where was my sister?

I had to tell someone about the mistake, and I looked at my family lined around the coffin. "Moma, Dad, it's not—that's not—"

My father patted me on the shoulder just as a surge of visitors came through the door. I saw our neighbor Mrs. Merritt, the one Mog and I always called Mrs. Halitosis, bearing down on me. She backed me into a spray of gladiolus, leaning toward me so that her breath hit my face in little puffs as she said, "Oh, that poor, poor girl."

I meant to say that it was a terrible mix-up, that it had never happened. Instead I said, "She doesn't have her shoes on."

Streams of people came all afternoon: friends and relatives, and some we'd never seen before. We went home for supper but were back by seven. And the crowd grew so, the man in the black suit pushed open a folding wall into another room.

Sister Leonard arrived just before nine o'clock, bringing the roses from the senior class. "I sent the girls off to their graduation parties—against their wishes, but I sent them," she said, her arms around my mother. "But they'll all be here tomorrow. And for the funeral."

"Graduation?" my mother said, shaking her head.

Mog's friends from St. Kit's were there most of Monday, staying for a while, leaving, then coming back. They huddled around the coffin, crying and clinging to one another. They surrounded my mother, and she smiled at them with her plastic face and gave them air kisses and didn't see them.

Father Nichols came in the evening and was just about to gather us together for a prayer service when a silence rolled across the room. I looked up to see Bobby Ritter standing in the doorway. His arm was in a cast and a sling; his face was ashen. His mother and father, one on each side, were sort of holding him up without actually touching him. Everyone was looking at him, and for a minute the whole scene was like a video that has been put on stop.

Then my mother sailed across the room, catching him by his good arm and making him wince. Her voice was high as she said, "Oh, Bobby, it would mean so much if tomorrow, at the funeral, we walked together. You and I."

The silence in the room deepened. I wanted to scream, "No, you can't do this to him," but my voice was locked somewhere inside of me. I looked around, willing someone to put an end to this. My father's face was twisted in pain—but he didn't speak. Cricket kicked at the carpet underfoot, and Reilly opened her mouth and closed it again. Nana stepped forward and put her hand on Moma's arm, but my mother shook her away.

"Bobby?" she said.

Finally—hours, days, maybe weeks later—Mr. Ritter inched closer to Bobby and said, "We're so sorry, Clara. You and your family have our deepest sympathy. If there's ever anything we can do—" He stopped for a moment before going on. "But Bobby's here against all medical advice, and if he's even able to come tomorrow it would be better if he sat in the back with his mother and me." And slowly, carefully, he steered Bobby over to the coffin as little conversations started up again throughout the room.

A few minutes later I saw the Ritters going out. I ran after them, following them into the hall, calling, "Bobby, wait."

He turned and came toward me and we stood holding each other as best we could, what with him with one arm tied up and me trying not to hurt him. There were a bunch of things we didn't say, but in an odd way it was as if we *did* say them. At least, for me it was. And I hope for Bobby, too.

The funeral went by in a kind of blur. We sang the eagle's wings song and "How Can I Keep from Singing?" and I remember thinking that Mog would've liked that. Father Nichols talked about how he'd known her all her life and told a story of the time, years ago, when he came for dinner, and Mog and I had frozen dirty dishwater in the ice trays to see what would happen, and we found out all right. Everybody laughed—even though it was a funeral. Then Brooke and Allison read a poem they'd written about how the three of them had been best friends since kindergarten, and they managed to make it almost to the end without crying. And the whole time that they were reading I sat next to Cricket, wondering how he was holding up, and thinking of a bunch of things I wanted to tell Mog and knowing there was no way I would be able to say them. Not with everyone looking on like that.

From the church we went to the cemetery, where we stood on a hill under a green tent surrounded by the graves of dead Fitzhughs. The coffin hung suspended over a giant gaping hole and I closed my eyes to keep from seeing it. But I saw it anyway. I opened my eyes and looked beyond the friends and family circled around us, past the marble angels and crosses and lambs, to the city streets crowding against the walls. I wanted to run. Just then the man in the black suit tapped me on the arm and motioned to a folding chair. I shook my head at him and went to stand behind it, steadying myself for a minute, still thinking of escape.

Father Nichols shook holy water on the coffin, and for a minute I watched it glimmer as it caught in the yellow roses on top. He said a prayer. He cleared his throat and turned away for a minute. Then he turned back and said that the family would like everyone to join them at the house. And when he was finished I felt as though I'd been holding my breath for a long, long time.

And that was it. We turned and made our way down the hill to where the cars were parked. The man in the black suit opened the door to the limo and my mother got in, followed by Reilly and Cricket.

"Annie?" said Dad, touching me on the arm.

But I turned and ran, up the hill again, dodging tombstones, tripping over a bronze butterfly and almost falling, catching myself and going on. I moved in close to the coffin, slipping my fingers under the flowers and feeling the polished wood. "Mizpah, Mog," I said. Then I whispered the words, "The Lord watch between me and thee . . ." as I started toward the car, and for the first time in that long, horrible weekend I began to think that now maybe Mog and I were, in a way, absent one from the other.

Afterward, back at the house, people crowded into the first floor, spilling out onto the porches, into the yard. The table in the dining room was heaped with food that, during the afternoon, disappeared and was somehow always replenished. And over all there was the soft hush of voices. In one of those weird moments frozen in time, I felt as though I were part of a painting called *Guests at the Funeral Feast*. Except that all of a sudden Tommy and Clark came racing down the front stairs, chasing Homer through the hall, the living room, dodging men and women holding teacups, ducking under the dining room table, before heading into the kitchen and up the back stairs.

As if we had been set free, everyone sighed. Somebody laughed. Allison came in carrying a tray and calling, "Dove Bars, get your Dove Bars." Reilly kicked her shoes under the dictionary stand and retrieved a pair of flip-flops from somewhere. And Cricket went upstairs and came down in a pair of cutoffs and his Orioles T-shirt.

The only other thing I remember about that afternoon was that as she was leaving, Sister Leonard put her arm around me and told me that I wouldn't have to take my exams, that the teachers would grade me on my year-long work.

I did though, the following week. Take the exams, I mean. Because I couldn't think of what else to do.

It didn't rain for my graduation. The sun shone. St. Kit's looked beautiful. And we, the seniors, tried to seem spontaneous and unrehearsed and like wood nymphs in our all-different white dresses as we made our way through the crowd to our seats. From the platform, Sister Leonard beamed encouragingly.

I knew, without knowing how I knew it, that the only way to get through the rest of the day was to concentrate on what was happening at that very minute, to hold tight to my thoughts and never let them slide away. I listened hard to the music and stared at the grass and watched an ant crawl onto the toe of my shoe. I studied the label of Alice Ewell's dress sticking out of her collar and followed a cloud shaped like a camel as it drifted across the sky. And I was probably the only person there who paid attention to the woman judge's graduation speech all the way through, every last "salt of the earth" and "hope of the future" and "out into the world." I mean, if my father was the Cliché King of 4B, she could definitely have been a Potentate.

I crossed my fingers and hoped not to fall flat on my face when I went up to get my diploma.

Six

I had applied for a lifeguard job so late I almost didn't get one, but then Mr. Parker, the manager of Hopkins House, called and said the girl they'd hired was leaving for Europe and if I was still available he could use me around the middle of June. With nothing special to do until then, those first few days after graduation were long and flat and seemed to stretch out around me. Nana and Popoo had offered to take me home with them for a visit, but I said no, then wished I hadn't as soon as their car pulled away from the curb and swung around the corner at the end of the block. Erin had left for a trip to the Grand Tetons with her family, and Rachel and Chris and Nancy and just about everyone else I knew had headed to the beach—for a summer of waiting tables and living on their own.

I could've gone with them, I guess. I mean, Moma and Dad would have argued some but probably would have given in eventually. Only I never bothered to go down for interviews or team up with anyone for an apartment. Same as I never bothered to apply to college.

"I don't think so . . . maybe later . . . I'll go next year . . ." I mumbled when people asked about college, and the weird thing was that nobody said anything. Except for Reilly. And for Ms. Hart, the guidance counselor at St. Kit's, who totally freaked out and sent for applications: to Barnard (because that's where Mog had been planning to go), to Loyola, here in town (in case I wanted to be a commuter), and to Mount St. Mary's in Emmitsburg (because it was small and rather worn and comfortable-looking and she thought I might feel at home there). She called me into her office and for the next several days walked me through the essays and all the forms. The trouble was that when the letters came I never answered them: never accepted any of the acceptances.

So, while waiting for my job to begin, I would sit on the corner of the porch with my feet on the railing and Ben the cat in my lap, trying to make my mind a blank as my father went off to work ("Back to the grindstone," he'd say every morning), Cricket finished out the school year, and Moma created fantastic new birthday parties for all the five-year-olds who were turning six.

After a few days of my just sitting, Reilly turned herself into a committee of one to rescue me. She took me places. To the Pennsylvania Dutch country to look at quilts and downtown to the Women's Exchange for chicken sandwiches, because, as she said, the place was an anachronism. To the Peabody Institute Library, the Cross Street Market, and, along with about seventy million school kids, the Aquarium.

It was while we were at the aquarium that I saw her.

We had been to the dolphin show, then stopped to see the stingrays, the electric eels, the octopus, and had worked our way up to the third level and were looking at the puffins when I caught her reflection in the glass. I spun around just as she herded a group of children into the crowd, her long blond hair swinging in a single braid down her back. "Wait," I called. "Wait!"

And I ran after her, fighting my way past teachers and children wearing name tags, through knots of people making fish eyes at the giant grouper, and into the Captain's Cove. I saw her bend over and lift a sea star out of the water and show it to a boy in a striped T-shirt. "Wait," I called again. "You there, in the green dress. Mog—"

She looked up at me, and I caught my breath. "I'm sorry," I said. "I thought—I thought you were someone else."

And when I turned away, Reilly was there.

"I saw her reflection in the glass and thought— She looked just like— I was sure she was Mog," I said as Reilly led me up the escalator to the rain forest, where the humidity settled down around us.

"I know, I know," she said, patting me on the arm.

We didn't say much more until we had left the aquarium and walked around the harbor and were seated at a table, waiting for our lunch. "There's something about eating outdoors," said Reilly, squinting up at the sky, then digging in her bag for her sunglasses. "When George was alive we used to plan our vacations according to whether we could eat outside. I think that's why I liked Italy so much. And Mexico. Did I ever tell you about the time, in Acapulco, when George was so busy looking around that he walked into a pool and disappeared straightaway?"

"What happened?" I asked.

"Oh, he surfaced again and scrambled out, feeling like a fool, and we walked around for a while trying to dry him out. But I must say he squished a bit when we finally went to dinner, and when he paid the check the money was still soggy."

She sat for a minute without saying anything and smiling a faraway smile. Then she leaned forward, putting her hand on my arm. "That business at the aquarium—it works that way sometimes," said Reilly. "You go somewhere and see someone and you're so sure, and then—But it does get better, Annie, except, well, I've been thinking that maybe now it's time for some professional help." She held a basket of rolls out to me.

I shook my head at her, not at the rolls *or* the idea of professional help, but because I was suddenly too angry to speak: angry at some perfect stranger because she wasn't Mog, and at Mog for not being the stranger. And then, maybe for the first time ever, I knew that Reilly's chamomile tea and Band-Aids weren't going to be enough.

And when we got home, I went back to my corner of the porch, as I did after every outing. Only today the thoughts rushed in: of the girl in the aquarium and how I'd followed her, and in a way it made me think of how I'd followed Mog my whole life long, doing everything she had done, only two years later. How I'd gone ahead with graduation because I didn't know any way *not* to. And how now I was suddenly stranded, without Mog to show me the way, more alone even than I'd been two years before.

I tried to ignore those thoughts but instead felt myself being sucked into that other time.

The days after Mog's funeral had been long and flat, too. Once my exams were over, Reilly put me to work helping to write thank-you notes, and the two of us would sit at the kitchen table working our way through the list, checking addresses, licking stamps. At the start, I tried to make every note different, to really *say* something, but after a while I gave up and fell into a pattern, changing it only to "the wonderful casserole," "the lovely flowers," "the thoughtful mass card."

From time to time Moma would come into the kitchen, to get an iced tea or take out something to thaw for dinner, but she never asked what we were doing and always managed to look somewhere just over our heads. Because in the game my mother was still playing, what had happened hadn't. The thing I didn't really understand, though, was that if it had never *happened,* and if Mog wasn't *here,* then did Moma think she'd never *existed?* Moma's behavior was so completely bizarre that I needed to talk to Mog about it. Which was maybe even more bizarre.

When the notes were sent, the casserole dishes, cake plates, and brownie tins returned, I was suddenly out of things to do. I talked to Erin on the phone and went out to her house whenever I could talk Moma, or Reilly, or Dad into taking me there. I walked down to Video Americain on Cold Spring Lane and brought home tearjerker movies and cried for make-believe people. I put up a BABY-SITTER

AVAILABLE notice on the bulletin board at Eddie's, but most of the kids in the neighborhood went to day camp. Besides, after the rush at the time of the funeral, people seemed to start pulling away from us, as if they'd decided that because of what had happened to Mog we were somehow tainted. As if murder didn't happen in "nice" families. I went to the pool with Cricket, and when he went off with his friends I sort of hogged the lap lane and swam and swam until I couldn't swim anymore.

Mostly, though, I pored over the newspaper, starting with the front page and working my way through the Maryland section and onto the back page, sure that the *Sun* would keep running stories about Mog's death, about the investigation. But new murders and a series of accidents and a kidnapping had taken their place.

Detective Leggett, from the Homicide Division, came to the house twice; both times Moma excused herself and went upstairs. He stood in front of the fireplace in the living room, leaning on the mantel, which was cluttered with Grandma Fitzhugh's collection of china elephants, a weathered bird's nest, pictures of Mog, Cricket, and me, each in our First Communion clothes, and a candlestick without any candles, and told us that the investigation was continuing. And then, almost as an afterthought, he added that they had nothing to go on: no fingerprints, no footprints caught in mud, the way they do in Agatha Christie novels, no easy clues dropped at the scene of the crime.

Once, a week or so after the detective's last visit, I heard my father on the phone to him and listened shamelessly outside the door while he almost groveled for information: "There must be something you can tell me . . .

some way you can . . ." And I heard the defeat in his voice as he said, "I understand . . . I'm sure you are . . . Thank you."

Thank you. I wanted to rage. *Thank you* for what? For letting Mog's killer run loose? For giving up and going on to other things? For leaving him out there, free to do to someone else what he had done to Mog?

I was still in the hall when Dad came out. He stood for a minute, shaking his head, before he said, "They're doing their best, Annie. I've got to believe that."

About this time I began to look over my shoulder as I walked down the street, to come in off the porch at the first hint of darkness, to jump at every creaky floorboard. I took to closing my windows at night, huddling back in my bed as the sweat ran in rivulets and my pillow grew damp, because, according to the family fiction, our house was big and shady and didn't need air-conditioning. The windows were always open again in the morning, and one night I forced myself out of a deep sleep to see my father raising them. When he was done he turned and, touching me lightly on the cheek, whispered, "It's all right, Annie," before he tiptoed out of the room.

One night in July I noticed that the door to Mog's room was ajar. I pushed it open and went in and found Cricket, sitting on the floor and leaning back against the bed, listening to a Bruce Springsteen CD.

"Hey," I said, "why don't you take them?"

"Take what?"

"The CD player. And all the CDs. Why don't you take them to your room?" I said.

He looked at me as if waiting for the punch line. "They're Mog's."

"Yeah, but now—not . . . Anyway, they're just sitting here. And besides, she'd like for you to have them."

"How do you know?" he asked.

"I just do, is all."

"Did she say so? Did she ever?"

Yeah, sure, I wanted to shout. Moggie and I always sat around planning our last wills and testaments. It ranked right up there with did we like the mountains better than the shore and what to do with the rest of our lives. I opened my mouth to say all that but caught myself, watching as Cricket leaned forward, his face intent, his forehead crinkled.

"She did," I said, not even bothering to cross my fingers. "We were talking once about—you know—what'd ever happen if— And she said it right out, how she wanted you to have the CDs, the player, the receiver, and anything else. How about her new tennis racket. The—"

"No," he said. "Just the music." Then, after a minute, he jerked his head in the direction of Moma and Dad's room. "What about them?"

"It'll be okay, don't worry," I said. "Now come on, let's move this stuff into your room." I stopped the music and unplugged and unhooked everything, picking up the receiver and one of the speakers and starting for the door, calling back, "Grab the rest. And there're more CDs in the closet."

I kicked open the door to Cricket's room and caught my breath. "Yuck, what're you growing in here?"

"It's an unscientific study," he said, coming along behind me. "The effects of heat and humidity on pepperoni pizza."

"Yeah, well, it could be dangerous to your health." I

stood holding the receiver, looking around the room, trying to decide where to put it. I finally set it on the foot of
the bed next to a pair of grungy tennis shoes and the little
TV from the kitchen. "Maybe if you got rid of the beer
cans," I said, eyeing the shelves between the windows.
"Besides, I don't think people *collect* beer cans anymore."

"I don't collect them—I bought them all from Roger's
brother and he says they'll be valuable someday. Here, I'll
make a place." And he took his elbow and swept the top of
the desk clean, sending books and pencils, a backpack,
lacrosse balls, and a 1945 license plate onto the floor. He
retrieved the receiver and put it in the middle of the desk,
lining the boxes of compact discs next to it. When I left he
was crawling around on the floor, looking for the outlet.
And by the time I got back to my room the sound of Bruce
Springsteen's voice filled the second floor.

Later that night, Dad was in the kitchen when I went
down to get something to drink. Quickly, without stopping to think and before I could lose my nerve, I said,
"What about Mog's things? I mean, what should we do
with them?"

"Ask your mother," Dad said. "She may have—"

"My mother's out to lunch," I flared back. "Even when
she's home she's out to lunch."

"Well, now, Annie, I'm sure she'll be all right, I'm sure
she's dealing with this as best she can."

And I wanted to yell back at him that to be all right you
have to know something is *wrong,* but he looked so beaten
down that I just said, "What do *you* think I should do
with them?"

"Whatever people do," he said, calling Homer for his
late night walk.

And it wasn't till after he had left that I realized that that was why I had asked in the first place: I didn't *know* what people did.

Reilly did, though, and the next day, when no one else was home, we went through Mog's clothes, clearing dresser drawers and closet shelves, sorting, packing. And the whole time we were doing it I put my mind in the "off" position, trying not to think, not to feel.

"Don't you want this?" or "That color would do well for you," she'd say from time to time, holding up a sweater, a shirt, a pair of shorts. And each time I'd shake my head and watch as she dropped whatever it was into one of the leaf bags lined along the side of the bed. We put Mog's scrapbooks and pictures and letters and old school papers in boxes and stored them in the closet. We set aside her silver locket and a couple of bracelets for the cousins and her collection of earrings for Allison and Brooke. And at the last minute I unstuck the Picasso poster from the wall and carried it over to my room, hanging it opposite the bed and taping over the scraps of tape already there, because somehow they had to do with Mog.

When we were done we carried the bags outside and bundled them into Reilly's car, and later that afternoon she drove off with them lined along the backseat, like children going to the fair.

"Dinner, Annie," I heard my father call. "Your mother has dinner ready."

I tried to pull myself back into the present, looking around the porch and rubbing my eyes. "Will they ever catch him?" I said.

"No," he said. "If they were going to—if they could

have—it would have been right away, I think." He sighed and turned away, picking at a paint blister on the railing. "I'm very much afraid that this is all we can expect."

Later that night, as I stood in my room trying to keep from feeling I was slipping into cold dark water, I rooted through the basket on my dresser, searching for the card Erin's mother had given me, the one from the woman she thought maybe could help. I found it folded in with my graduation program and a carry-out menu from Uncle Lee's and took it over to the window, rubbing my fingers over it, reading the name out loud. Harriet Jeffers, LCSW.

Seven

When I called the next morning, I thought that Harriet Jeffers would be waiting at the other end of the line for me: that she would tell me to come right over and make me cocoa, the way Erin's mom had, and offer me distractions, the way Reilly sometimes did. And that suddenly everything would be okay.

Instead, when I worked up the nerve to call her, I got an answering service. And a generic person who said that if I left my name and number, Ms. Jeffers would get back to me.

"When?" I wanted to ask, but didn't. I took a deep breath and gave her the message in a voice that sounded small and wimpy and not at all like anyone Harriet Jeffers would probably ever want to talk to.

Afterward I sat staring at the phone, willing it to ring. I gave up eventually and ran down to the cellar to move my clothes from the washer to the dryer, hurrying all the way so I wouldn't miss the call. And when Cricket and Roger Carmody came in and got on the phone, trying to scare up people for a softball game, I bribed them with money for ice cream cones from Baskin-Robbins and practically shoved them out the door.

Once they were gone, the silence in the house was deafening, and I glared at the phone hanging on the wall like some fat green frog. And for a minute it seemed to glare back at me. Finally, when I was just finishing my lunch, the call came.

"This is Harriet Jeffers," she said. "Am I speaking to Annie?"

"Yes," I said, and then, after what seemed like hours, figured out that I was supposed to keep going. I started and stopped and started again, and heard myself speaking in that same small, wimpy voice. "This is Annie. Annie Fitzhugh. And I got your name from my friend Erin's mother. That's Erin McNabb, and Mrs. McNabb. And I'd like to—I need to—I think maybe I want to make an appointment."

"Well, now, Annie," said Harriet Jeffers, "what kind of an issue is it that you want to work on?"

"Oh, you know—just a lot of things. I mean, I graduated from high school a couple of weeks ago, and everybody—all my friends know where they're going and what they're doing, and they're heading off to college and I'm not. Mostly because I couldn't get myself together to apply, except that Ms. Hart, the guidance counselor, forced me into it, only then I never did anything about the acceptances."

I hated the way I was babbling, and kept right on doing it. "And now things are crowding me and pulling away both at the same time and sometimes at night I'm afraid and I close the windows and then—and now— Oh, I don't know."

"Okay, Annie. Have you told your parents that you want to see a therapist?"

"No, but they won't care. Well, they'll *care,* but they won't mind. My dad anyway."

"And your mom?"

"My mom's—well, it's complicated, and hard to explain."

Harriet Jeffers didn't say anything for a moment, as if she was listening to what I wasn't saying. Then she went on about medical insurance and how I should bring my card when I came. She asked if I was working this summer, and when she heard I'd be starting next week she said that an early morning appointment, before the pool opened for the day, would probably be better. We settled on the following Wednesday.

It wasn't until I'd hung up that I realized that I hadn't mentioned Mog.

That night, when Dad set out with Homer for his before-bedtime walk, I went with him. We headed up the street toward Roland Avenue, talking about how hot it was for June and watching the way the humidity hung over the streetlights, making them look fuzzy and somewhat distant. When we got to the corner, Homer turned around and started home, but I caught hold of the leash, taking it out of my father's hand and saying, "Wait, could we go back the long way. There's something I want to ask you."

"Sure," said Dad. "What's on your mind?"

"It's that, well, Mog's been dead for two years now, and sometimes I think I'm still as much a mess as I was then. And I'd like to see a therapist. If that's okay."

"Of course it's okay," said Dad. "It's more than okay." He waited while Homer sniffed all sides of a fire hydrant. Then he said, "And one thing's for certain: if I had it to do over again, I'd've gotten us all into counseling right after Mog was killed."

"Especially Moma," I said, almost without knowing I was going to say it.

"Especially your mother," he said. A bus went by and Dad watched until it was almost out of sight before saying, "I guess I really did think that time would heal all wounds. That if we waited long enough . . . Anyway, we'll call Dr. Stringer and see if he can recommend someone for you."

"I have someone," I said. "A name, a card. Erin's mother gave it to me when I spent the night after the party before graduation. I have an appointment for next week, only she said I should tell you and see about insurance and all." I stopped, hearing the words I'd said and trying to think how to sort them out. "I don't mean *should* tell you, because I would've told you anyway. Wanted to. And it's not that Erin's mother was being nosy or anything. She just gave me the card in case I ever needed it, and I decided I did."

My father didn't say anything for so long that I began to get worried. Finally he cleared his throat a couple of times and said, "I'm glad she did, Annie. And, come to think of it, Ellie McNabb started to tell me at graduation that she was concerned about you, but there was so much commotion, so many people coming up and interrupting, that we never really got a chance to talk. Now I feel as if I have two left feet, or fumbled the ball, or—"

I laughed and made a face, which he probably couldn't see in the dark, and said, "That teacher was right, Dad. The one when you were in 4B."

He ignored me, though, and went on. "This therapist? Who is she?"

"Harriet Jeffers, with a LCSW after her name. Whatever that means."

"Licensed certified social worker," said Dad.

"And what about Moma?" I asked. "What'll she think?"

"Don't worry about your mother, I'll talk to her. Though I can't say for sure what her reaction'll be, or whether she'll even acknowledge it." He sighed and put his arm around my shoulders as we started up the walk to the house.

I guess none of us could have guessed what Moma's reaction would be—if, in fact, what happened the next day really was brought on by Dad telling her I wanted to see a therapist. We'll probably never know for sure. Anyway, I managed to piece it together from Reilly, who was there, and from what I found when I came in from the dentist.

Cricket had finished lunch and headed outside to cut the grass, which is his job as of this year, especially since he's gone into the lawn care business and uses our mower all around the neighborhood. "Charity begins at home," Dad told him when he grumbled a bit. "Either that or fair's fair. Take your pick."

Reilly was at the kitchen table working on her crossword puzzles, doing two at once as she always does, her pencil hopping around the page.

Moma was sitting across from her, planning a scavenger hunt for Aimee Walter's birthday party. As Reilly remembers it, she had just asked Moma if she knew a four-letter Turkish weight when, without answering her and almost as if she were in a trance, my mother got up and drifted out of the room, leaving her half-eaten sandwich and unopened Coke.

Reilly went back to her puzzle and didn't pay any attention until she heard thumpings and bumpings from upstairs. Even then she just looked at the ceiling for a few minutes and concentrated on trying to finish off the quote in 48 across. That was because it was Friday and, as Reilly said, the puzzles are always harder on Fridays.

In a while, though, the noises grew louder and more frantic. Doors slammed, and there was the sound of something being dragged overhead. Walls vibrated; the whole house seemed to shudder. Reilly had just gotten up to go investigate when I came in the back door. And together we heard the crash.

We ran up the stairs, squeezing past a marble-topped dresser that was swung across the hall, climbing over a rocking chair lying on its side, and stepping around my wicker tray table and a teddy bear with a missing ear. We found Moma on the stairway to the attic, wedged between the wall and an oak headboard. "Tell Cricket I need him," she said.

I reached for the headboard, but before I could get hold of it Moma had righted herself and was thumping it down the steps. "Get Cricket," she said, her voice tight and shrill. "I want this bed put together *now*."

"I'll get him and be right back," said Reilly, resting her hand on my arm for a minute. "See if you can figure out what's going on here."

I followed Moma into Mog's room, where she dropped the headboard with a terrible clatter and started for the door.

"Moma, wait. What are you doing?"

She didn't answer me and I ran after her, up the narrow stairs and into the attic, where the heat slammed down against us. I watched as she crawled under the eaves and came out dragging a bundle of bed slats. Downstairs, she dropped them onto the bed and darted into the guest room, pushing and pulling at an old washstand, forcing it into the hall, where the pitcher that had been teetering on top fell to the floor, the china shattering and spraying into the corners.

She turned away from that and went into my room. Then she grabbed the wire birdcage off the windowsill and came back to the hall just as Cricket ran up the stairs, with Reilly panting behind him.

"Hey, what's going on here?" he asked.

"I want this room put back," Moma said, her arms still wrapped around the birdcage. "The way it was."

"But, Moma, it *is* the way it was," I said. "The way Mog left it. You know, simple and monastic."

"That was just a phase," my mother said. "A passing fancy." She put the birdcage on top of the bookcase and picked up the headboard, propping it against the wall and reaching for one of the side pieces, trying to fit them together.

"But what's the point?" said Cricket.

"I want this room put back," my mother said in a voice so low that I had to strain to hear it. "I want Mog back."

For a long time nobody moved, and then, without looking at each other, Cricket and I took the pieces out of

Moma's hands and Reilly picked up the footboard. Moma, her face glossy with sweat and her eyes wild and unfocused, flattened herself against the wall and watched us.

After a while she darted out the door, and I heard her go down the hall to Cricket's room. In a few minutes she was back, her arms filled with boxes of compact discs. She dumped them on the mattress and hurried off again. When she came back she was struggling with the receiver and the CD player, kicking one speaker along in front. "These are *hers.* Mog's," she said as she unloaded them onto the desk.

Cricket gasped and stepped back as if he had been slapped.

"No, Moma! No!" I cried, turning toward her, taking hold of her hands and leaning close. "Mog's gone, and these belong to Cricket now. It's been two years. Besides, she wanted it that way. And all the beds and CDs and birdcages, even that ratty old teddy bear, won't bring her back. She's dead."

My mother howled and pulled away from me. She ran down the hall and through her room, into the bathroom, slamming the door and locking it. I stood outside, my ear pressed against the wood, listening as the shower came on full force. And my mother's sobs suddenly seemed louder than anything I'd heard before.

Cricket, Reilly, and I cleaned up the mess. We finished putting the bed together, because it was easier than dragging it back to the attic, and hoisted the box spring and mattress onto the frame. We moved the marble-topped dresser under the window in the hall and shoved the washstand back to the guest room, then set the rocker in the corner of Mog's room. With the teddy bear on it. I left the birdcage where it was, for the time being at least, but gathered up the stereo stuff and carried it into Cricket's room.

"I don't want it," he said, coming after me and leaning against the doorjamb. I pretended I didn't hear him and crawled in back of the desk to hook everything up.

Then I turned and sat on the floor, trying to ignore the gunk growing all around me. "A fungus amongus," I said, pulling in my arms and legs.

"Yeah," said Cricket, as he pushed an empty Coke can with a blackened banana peel draped over the top out of the way and sat down next to me.

"Remember when Dad used to say that when we were little and he wanted us to clean our rooms?"

"That was heavy," said Cricket.

"What? A fungus amongus?"

"No, *that,* you know, Moma. That whole thing."

"Heavy *and* scary."

"Heavy and *scary.*"

"Weird."

"But the thing I don't get," said Cricket, scrunching forward. "The thing is—with Moma—she knows about Mog . . ."

"Knows she's dead."

"Knows she's dead—but it's like she doesn't *really* know. Like there's some huge gigantic thing between what she knows and what she— And it keeps us from—" He stopped and shook his head and shoved his fingers through his hair, already streaked by the sun. "Sometimes I want to *talk* about Mog, out loud, at the dinner table or someplace. Like she was still a part of our family. Like she was still here."

"*We* could, you know. Talk about her, I mean."

"Yeah," said Cricket, sighing. "We could."

We didn't, though, not right then anyway, but the funny thing was that the air around us was easier to breathe and the grunge in Cricket's room seemed to creep back and give us space.

After a while we got up and went down the hall, where Reilly was straightening the books in the bookcase, and together the three of us stood looking at Mog's room—which wasn't Mog's room anymore, wasn't the way she left it or even the way it used to be before she made it monastic. And was now just a room.

When I went into the kitchen before dinner, Moma was cutting up squash and listening to "All Things Considered." I stood in the doorway watching her for a minute, thinking that she looked the way she always looked, was acting the way she always acted. And that if I hadn't seen it myself, if Reilly and Cricket hadn't seen it, I'd never have believed this was the same woman who, just a few hours earlier, had ransacked the house and stood sobbing in the shower. If anything, the plastic that she'd shrouded herself in over the last two years was thicker than ever.

But if Moma was laminated, the rest of us certainly weren't and dinner was painful. Even for Dad, because I'd seen Reilly talking to him as he came up the walk and was sure she'd told him what had happened. For once Cricket remembered everything he'd been told about not putting his elbows on the table or reaching or talking with his mouth full. Reilly drummed her fingers on the side of her iced-tea glass and threw out bits of conversation that the rest of us never managed to catch hold of, so that they just lay there like strands of seaweed washed up along the shore. Dad watched Moma, while pretending not to. And I waited for dinner to be over and planned my escape.

But Cricket beat me to it. No sooner had he carried his dishes into the kitchen than he announced he was going to Roger's and was it okay if he spent the night and he'd see us in the morning. Reilly suddenly remembered a book she needed at the library. Moma tried out the clues to Aimee Walter's scavenger hunt on Dad, and then they both went in to watch the news on CNN. And I got stuck with the dishes.

The thing about dishes in our house is that they always get done. Eventually. I mean, there isn't any schedule about who does what when, and the only rule is that the person who cooks doesn't have to clean up. For the most part everybody pitches in. Except that night, when I found myself alone in the kitchen with Homer. And he obviously wasn't going to help.

"That's okay, boy," I said, stepping over him to get to the dishwasher. "Just let me finish up here and we'll go for a walk." And at the word *walk* he moved to the back door, stretching out in front of the sill so I wouldn't leave without him.

When the dishes were done I ran upstairs to get some money, calling into the den as I came down, "I'm taking Homer and we're going for ice cream. Okay?" Then I hurried into the kitchen, grabbing the dog's leash and hooking it on, heading out before anyone could stop me or offer to come along.

All the way to Baskin-Robbins, I told Homer about Moma and what had happened this afternoon and how if I hadn't gotten out of the house I'd probably have exploded. Part of the time I pretended he was Harriet Jeffers; part of the time I was glad he wasn't.

When I turned off the avenue onto the parking lot, I almost fell over Bobby Ritter. He was sitting on the curb, eating an ice cream cone.

Eight

"Homer!" cried Bobby Ritter, lunging for the dog just as the dog lunged for him. I dropped the leash and there was a whirlwind of arms and legs, slobber and barks, until I felt as if I were looking through a kaleidoscope gone askew. The scene slowly came into focus as Homer sat back on his haunches and ate the ice cream cone Bobby held out to him.

"Hi, Annie," said Bobby, wiping his hands on his pants.

"Hi, Bobby." I sat down next to him. "Guess I owe you an ice cream."

"No way. I gave it to him. Homer's my buddy. I've missed him. I've missed you all."

"Yeah, well, we're there. We think about you, ask about you." And because I seemed to be wandering into a conversational dead end I stood up and said, "If you hold the dog I'll go in and get a couple of cones."

"Okay," he said, reaching into his pocket and handing me some money. "I guess chocolate for me this time. It's not good for dogs, so I won't be tempted to share it with him."

When I came out, Homer was lying on his back with his feet in the air and Bobby was rubbing him under the chin.

"I mean it about missing him. Our dog died last year, and with my sister married and me away at college, my mother replaced him with a cat, who's okay except that he seems to have a foot fetish. If I so much as twitch my toes under the covers he attacks them."

I laughed for a minute and then said, "Come over sometime and play ball with him. Remember how you used to do that for absolute ages? You were the only person who could wear this dog out. Remember how he'd give up and go lie in the middle of the rose bed? Remember when— How's your arm?"

"Well, I'll never pitch major league ball, but then I'd never have pitched major league ball *anyway*. And after a bunch of operations it's okay. How are you, Annie?"

Something about the way Bobby asked, "How are you, Annie?"—leaning forward, so that his hair looked almost white in the streetlight—made me sort of dissolve. Without any warning, tears ran down my face.

"Hey, you can't eat and cry," he said, taking the ice cream cone out of my hand and dabbing at my face with a paper napkin.

"I'm okay now," I said, snuffling and swallowing hard and reaching for my cone. "It's just that my mother's a wacko and I'm going to see a shrink. And it's been *two years*."

"Two years, ten years, I don't think it matters. It happened and there's no way around it. I'm glad you're going to see someone."

"She's a LCSW. Does that count as a shrink?" I asked.

"Forget the labels," said Bobby, picking up the end of Homer's leash and rolling it tight. "It's how she works with *you* that counts. And if she doesn't—work well, I mean—then get another one. It's like shoes: you keep trying till you get the right fit."

"Did you see someone? Do you still?" I asked.

"Yeah, right away. When it happened. And now, too, only that's mostly for tune-ups. Because the insurance people think we should make do with quick cures. And it mounts up when your parents try to carry the bills on their own. We found that out the hard way. Now, what's this about your mother?"

"She's not really a wacko." I sighed. "I shouldn't have said that." And just as quickly as the tears had overtaken me, I started to giggle. "She's a driver's license."

Bobby stared at the ground between his feet, studying an ant pushing at a piece of cone. "Plastic-coated?" he said after a while.

"Yes," I said, suddenly sober. "Only this afternoon the plastic cracked and she totally freaked out and ran through the house, trying to turn Mog's room back into the way it used to be when we were little. And I could understand that, sort of. But afterward, tonight, it's as if it never happened. As if the plastic was miles thicker now."

"That's worse," said Bobby. "That shell keeping the pain at bay. I mean, if you hurt, if you allow yourself to hurt and somehow get through it, then it gets better and maybe there are bits of time when you can actually let it go. That's what they tell me anyway."

I was thinking about what Bobby had said when a car pulled up in front of us and a guy in a Yankees cap leaned out the window and called, "Hey, Ritter. Don't go anywhere. I want to talk to you."

We watched as he turned into a parking place, got out, and went into the store. "Who's that?" I said. "And why's he wearing a Yankees cap in Baltimore?"

"A guy I work with this summer, name's Amos. And he thinks he's confrontational. That's why the hat."

"Where do you work?" I asked.

"Down at Video Americain. The one in Charles Village. What about you?"

"I've got a lifeguard job at that apartment house on Thirty-ninth and University. It's mostly people from the building and the neighborhood and a few by-the-dayers. I won't know a soul, but it's a job, and since I waited till almost the last minute it was either that or walking around the food court at the mall with a squirt bottle and cleaning off tables. Yuck."

"That's an okay pool," said Bobby. "I went there a few times after work last summer. And I'll come again this year. So you'll know someone."

Just then Amos came up with what looked like a bucket of ice cream, holding it out to us and taking extra spoons from his pocket. "Help yourselves. I'm Amos, by the way," he said, turning to me. "That's a great dog."

"Oh, sorry," said Bobby, reaching for a spoon. "This is Annie—and the great dog's name is Homer Fitzhugh."

Amos sat down on the ground across from us and turned to Bobby. "I went by your house and your father said he thought you were up here. I wanted to see if you were interested in going over to the Film Forum. They're showing an early Bergman at nine-thirty. And you, too, Annie," he said, still holding the ice cream out to me.

"No thanks," I said, shaking my head at both the movie and the ice cream. "I'm going to get along home. Are you a Yankees fan, by the way?"

"No," said Amos. "It's just that a hat is a hat is a hat. Are you—a fan, I mean?"

"Of the Orioles, except that I'm not *really,* but my sister was. Even when she was little, Mog was such a fan that one time Reilly bought her a Walkman when it wasn't even her birthday or anything so she wouldn't miss any games and Cricket and I didn't even care because she was—"

I broke off and stood up, tugging on Homer's leash. "Anyway, we have to get on home."

"Wait just a minute and we'll give you a ride. Bobby and Homer in the backseat, you and me up front, okay?" He made Harpo Marx eyes and shoved his baseball cap around, front to back.

"Thanks anyway, but it's still light out and I'll be fine. Besides, I have Homer. But it was good meeting you. And come over, Bobby, when you get a chance."

"Annie . . ."

I heard Bobby start after me and I swung around, walking backward and shaking my head, calling, "No, really. I'm fine."

It was darker than I thought, though, especially when I got away from the lights of the parking lot, and for a minute I was tempted to change my mind. "No," I scolded myself, then "No," again. "It's fine. Hardly dark at all. And you're not far from home. A few blocks and—"

"But they're long blocks," I answered myself back.

"So what?" I shortened Homer's leash and held it taut.

When we turned off Roland Avenue the dark was even thicker, and I started to jog and then to run. I tripped over a break in the sidewalk and went down on one knee, letting out a yelp as Homer circled me, tangling me in his leash. I stayed that way for a minute, feeling the grit of the pavement under my hands and the dog's slobbery kisses as he licked my arms, my face. But the shadows seemed to threaten me, crouching closer and closer, and I scrambled to my feet.

I ran on, this time more carefully, picking my feet up high, and looking over my shoulder, trying to listen for noises over the thudding of my heart. A rabbit darting across a lawn spooked Homer and he danced at the end of his leash. A cloud slid in front of the moon. Somewhere in the distance a dog barked, and then another, and another, the sounds coming closer, as if to warn me that someone was out there, moving steadily toward me.

I spun around the corner onto my street, where things looked amazingly normal. I stopped to catch my breath before going on, waving to Mr. Clemens, who was pooper-scooping his yard by the light of the streetlamp.

Dad was standing on the front steps, and as soon as he saw me he looked up at the sky, pretending, I was sure, that he was checking on the weather and not waiting for me. "Okay?" he said as I went up the walk.

"No problem," I answered. "And Dad, guess who I saw at Baskin-Robbins? Bobby Ritter, and he's coming over someday to play ball with Homer."

When I woke the next morning three thoughts were bouncing around in my head, sort of battling one another for room. I tried to ignore them, concentrating instead on the squiggly crack on my ceiling. The one I always thought of as a giant peony bush ready to blossom—and that Mog said was actually a thunderstorm waiting to happen. But since I was the one who had to sleep under it, I always opted for the peony bush.

But the thoughts kept jiggling at me, poking and jabbing, so that I locked my hands behind my neck and looked up at the peony/thunderstorm, letting them wash over me.

One was how just plain comfortable it had been to see Bobby Ritter the night before.

Two was that if just the *idea* of my going to a therapist had caused Moma's outbreak, then maybe I shouldn't go to one.

And three was that, partly because of Moma's reaction and partly because of all the stuff rattling around inside of me, I was even surer than ever that I had to. See Harriet Jeffers, I mean.

Nine

Because Dad needed his car on Wednesday, he suggested I see if I could use Reilly's to get to my appointment with Harriet Jeffers, and that way Moma wouldn't have to be involved. How he really phrased it was "Why stir up a hornet's nest." And what he really *meant* was peace at any price.

It didn't seem right, however, especially since we've always been the kind of family who tell one another where we're going and when we'll be back, who leave Post-it notes stuck all over the kitchen counter saying "Home around 5," or "Gone to the library." Besides, the way I worked it out, if I was going to a therapist because I was having a problem dealing with Mog's death, and if part of the problem was that Moma *wasn't* dealing with it, then in order for me *to* deal with it I had to be open about it. Without being exactly "in your face" either. If that makes sense.

Casual and matter-of-fact, I told myself as I wandered into the kitchen, where Moma was cutting up chicken more or less in time to a tape of Wynton Marsalis playing baroque trumpet solos, which is what she listens to more than anything else, except maybe for Vivaldi's *Four Seasons* or Beethoven's Ninth. "Okay, then, I'm on my way," I said.

"To where?" said Moma, looking at me and raising her eyebrows.

"I have my first appointment with Harriet Jeffers this morning. You know, the therapist. Dad told you about her."

Moma flipped off the tape and concentrated on the chicken all of a sudden, carefully measuring spices, which was odd because she was the kind of cook who just threw a bunch of stuff together and stirred it up. And had it turn out.

I waited a minute to see if she was going to say anything. When she didn't, I took the keys off the board over the sink and called, "See you later," as I headed for the door.

So much for casual and matter-of-fact, I thought, climbing into the car and trying to keep my knees from shaking. My hands were clammy against the steering wheel, and there was a wobbly feeling in the pit of my stomach. The whole time I was on the Beltway, I kept having this mini interior debate—I will go . . . I won't . . . I will . . . I won't—and promising myself, at each exit, that I could get off and go home. But some part of my brain must have been on automatic pilot, because even as I was planning my escape I was following the directions I'd jotted down. And almost before I was ready, I was there, pulling into a parking place in front of Harriet Jeffers's office.

Except for her name on the outside door, there was nothing to tell me I was in the right place. No receptionist, no secretary, just a small empty room with a couch and a couple of chairs, and elevator music oozing out from the corners. At first I sat on the chair nearest the door. Next I moved over to the couch, leaning back for a minute, then forward to take a sour ball out of the bowl on the table. The paper crackled and roared as I unwrapped it. I was sure that electronic eyes were watching me, that hidden microphones were waiting to pick up whatever I might say. Or maybe even think.

And suddenly I was in any spy movie I had ever seen, Mata Hari, just waiting for someone else to come in, to sit down opposite me, so that together we could place identical folded newspapers on the table. In a few minutes I would stand and, oh so casually, pick up the wrong paper as I left. I was just spinning out this scenario when the inside door opened and a woman in a green-and-yellow muumuu said, "Hi, Annie, I'm Harriet Jeffers. Come on in."

"In" was down a hall to an office that was almost as impersonal as the waiting room, but not quite. There was a low-slung couch heaped high with pillows, two equally scrunchy chairs, and a round glass table with a Koosh ball and a box of Kleenex on top. I sat on the sofa, picking up the ball automatically and tossing it from one hand to the other so that it made a swirl of color in the air.

"Soothing, isn't it?" said Harriet Jeffers, settling into one of the chairs and drawing her legs up under her, wincing slightly. "Shingles," she said.

"Shingles?"

"Shingles, the disease. That's why I'm wearing the muumuu and wishing for the first time in my life I could join a nudist colony."

"Like Reilly," I said. "The shingles part, I mean. Not the nudist colony. She used to walk around with her arms out from her sides. From what I hear, shingles are really painful."

"Yes, well . . ." She shrugged and picked up a clipboard with a blank piece of paper on it. "Anyway, it's good to meet you, Annie. You mentioned when you called that there were some things bothering you, that you'd recently graduated and weren't clear about what you wanted to do next year. Is that right?"

"Yes," I said. I wanted to apologize for babbling on the phone, for my voice coming out small and wimpy, but then it occurred to me that apologizing for sounding small and wimpy was almost as bad as sounding that way. But I did it anyway. "I'm sorry for being such a ninny when I called the other day. It was just that—I mean I—and then . . ."

Harriet Jeffers ran her fingers through her short dark hair and grimaced. "Don't worry about it; everybody sounds that way. It's hard, you know, calling a perfect stranger you hope will help you sort a few things out, then spilling what it is that's bothering you, and still trying to hang on to a shred of dignity. Anyway, I'm Harriet, and you're Annie. Now let's get to work, okay?"

"Okay," I said, suddenly feeling so totally relaxed I was afraid I might topple over and fall asleep right there.

"Let me just get some background info, then," she said, her voice, both soothing and insistent, pulling me in.

"How about your general health, Annie? Has it been good?"

"Hmmmm, fine."

"Any problem with drugs or alcohol?"

I shook my head.

"Are you on any medication?"

"No."

"Your family doctor is . . . ?"

"Dr. Stringer, and except when I was little and used to get ear infections, I haven't had to see much of him."

"Good," said Harriet, jotting something on her piece of paper. "How about eating? Are you eating well?"

"Fine."

"Sleeping?"

"I wake up a lot."

"And then?"

"I'm afraid—and I close the window. And when I wake again, it's open."

"Do you know who opens it?"

I nodded. "My father."

"Is that okay?"

"Sure, because by then the sun is up and, besides, I'm hot and sweaty."

"Do you know why you're afraid?" Harriet asked. "What you're afraid *of*?"

The muscles in the back of my neck tensed and I shook my head, throwing the Koosh ball from hand to hand faster than ever. "No," I said.

"Well," said Harriet, "maybe we can get back to that." She swooped her pencil up the side of her paper and said, "I'd like it if you could tell me a little about your family.

On the phone you mentioned your father, your mother. How'd they feel about your coming here?"

"Fine. Dad, anyway."

"And your mother? Did you tell her, Annie?"

"Dad told her. And I told her, this morning, as I was leaving the house."

"How did she react?" Harriet asked.

"She didn't hear me." After a moment I shook my head so hard my earrings jangled and said, "She *heard* me, but she didn't. React, I mean. Except in a way I guess she did because she turned off the tape and concentrated on the chicken she was preparing as if at any minute it might self-destruct or something."

"And how did that make you feel?"

"I wanted to shake her," I said, putting my hand up to my mouth as soon as the words were out.

Harriet leaned back and waited for a minute before saying, "Let's talk about the rest of your family."

"There's Reilly," I said. "She's my father's cousin, well, mine, too, and she's great."

"What makes her great?"

"She just *is*, is all. I mean she's forever trying new things—she rode the subway the day it opened here in town, just for the heck of it, and last year she went hot-air ballooning. She's a retired librarian and old, sort of, but she doesn't act it, and she walks miles every day and reads and gardens and does Meals on Wheels. And the thing is, she's really with it without trying to act cool."

"And she lives with you?"

"Yes. Reilly always says she came with the house. It was Grandma and Granddad Fitzhugh's originally, and they left it to Dad and Moma and we all moved in and

Reilly was already there. That was just before Cricket was born."

"Cricket?"

"He's my brother. And he's fourteen now."

"Do you have any other brothers?"

"Just Cricket."

"Any sisters, Annie?"

"No," I said.

We sat without saying anything, Harriet looking down at the notes she had taken, me torturing the Koosh ball between my hands.

"Except for Mog," I said after a while.

"Mog?"

"Mog was my sister but now she's dead."

"Tell me about Mog, Annie," said Harriet, leaning slightly forward.

"She's dead."

"Was she older? Younger?"

"Older, by two years almost exactly. We were both born in October, Mog on the twenty-second and me on the seventeenth, so when we were little, every year during those five days we went around telling people we were just a year apart. Only now I've caught up, and starting with graduation, it's been as if I have to go on ahead—and I'm not sure I know the way."

"How did Mog die?" Harriet asked.

"She didn't just die—she was *murdered!*" I cried. I reached for a Kleenex, scrubbing at my face, then took another and shredded them both in my lap. Meanwhile, as if from far away, I heard Harriet saying something comforting, heard myself telling about the night of Jenny McNabb's party before Mog's graduation, about how she and Bobby Ritter went down to Fells Point afterward, so they could talk, and about the policemen who came to the house in the middle of the night.

"And when all the notes were written and the casserole dishes sent back and everything was over, there was Moma pretending that Mog hadn't died." I stopped for a moment to catch my breath. "And if Mog hadn't died, then the weird thing is that she couldn't have lived, and I began to think my sister had never happened except I . . ."

"Except I what, Annie?" said Harriet.

"Except I *know.*"

"Yes, good. But how do you know, Annie?"

"I just *do,* the way you know things. Besides, I remember."

"Ahhhh," Harriet said. "You remember."

"Yes. I have a million memories of Mog. I remember being in my crib with her on the outside handing things in. I remember the big yellow boots we both had and the day she started school and I didn't and how she brought a drawing home to me and the year she woke me at three in the morning so we could celebrate the exact minute of her birthday. I remember when her godparents gave her money for her First Communion and she bought me a Barbie, too, so we could both play, and how she'd come into my room at night and tell the most incredible ghost stories and go right back to her own room afterward without even having to turn the light on. I remember how sometimes we'd fight and not speak for a while and then we would again. Speak, I mean. I remember the Mizpah Picture and how even after we knew better we thought it was of us, and the time we were climbing Mr. Clemens's crab apple tree and I fell and cut my arm. Look, I still have the scar."

"You have your memories, then, and your scar. Anything else to tell you that Mog was here?"

"Cricket remembers. And Reilly and Dad and Bobby Ritter. Nana and Popoo and all the cousins. Brooke and Allison—even though they've gone on to college, they still remember. And Erin, and Sister Leonard from school."

"Okay," said Harriet. "You have other people's affirmations. Anything else?"

"Pictures," I said, digging in my wallet and pulling out a snapshot of Mog and me that was taken as we were coming out of the ocean down at Bethany the year before she died. I handed it to Harriet. "You can't really tell anything from this. We'd been swimming and her hair's all flattened down and she doesn't have her contacts in and can't see a thing and that's why she's squinting like that."

Harriet looked at the picture for a long time, nodding and smoothing the corners flat before giving it back. "Yes, yes," she said. And in a funny way that "Yes, yes" was exactly what I wanted her to say.

"How does your mother react to the pictures of Mog around the house?" Harriet asked.

"There aren't any."

"None? No baby pictures, nothing?"

"There were, and there still are—of me, and Cricket. But the others, the ones of Moggie—the little snapshots around the mirror in Moma's room, the ones in frames lined along the bookcases and on top of the player piano, even her eight-by-ten yearbook picture taken on the up end of a seesaw at school that hung on the picture wall in the den—are gone. And the thing is, I didn't know it was going to happen, didn't see them go, and one day, sometime after the funeral, they were just *gone.*"

"How did you feel when you saw they were missing?" Harriet asked.

"Scared, and lonely, and a little bit crazy. And one day when Moma was out at one of her birthday parties, because that's what she does, I rummaged through the house and found all the albums and boxes of photographs. I stuck one picture of the whole family, the way we used to be, on the inside of the lid of my jewelry box and hid the rest in the back of my closet so Moma couldn't take Mog all the way away.

"She can't, can she?

"She didn't, did she?"

Harriet looked at me for a long time before she said, "What do you think, Annie?"

And after another long time I shook my head and said, "No."

For the rest of the visit we pretty much talked about health insurance and how, before I came back next week, I was to write a description of a day in my life *now* and where I wanted to be in six months' time. And then, almost without knowing how I got there, I was in the car and sailing along the Beltway, on some kind of emotional high I hoped would never end.

Ten

I was still flying high when I got home. My feet scarcely hit the steps as I ran upstairs and then down again, changing into my bathing suit, packing lunch, grabbing a towel, finding the sunscreen, retrieving my book from where I'd left it under the porch swing the night before, and, finally, asking Reilly to give me a ride to work.

"How was it?" she said as we headed down Roland Avenue.

"Great," I said, and stopped, my hand halfway out to the radio dial. "I can't believe I said 'great.' As if I'd gone to a party or a rock concert or something and not to see a therapist because my sister—"

"Good, then," said Reilly. "Worthwhile."

I thought for a minute and said, "Lightening. As if something's been lifted a little. And the really strange thing is I don't know how she does what she does. I mean, she doesn't seem to *do* anything, no magic spells, nothing that I can put my finger on except . . ."

"She listens," said Reilly. "And probably in a constructive way. And knows what to say, what not to say."

"Hey, if it works I'll go with it. She can listen, or talk, or stand on her head, as long as she takes away what happened to Mog."

"No," said Reilly. She pulled up behind a UPS truck at a traffic light and turned to me, shaking her head. "No, Annie. Even the best therapist in the world can't take away what happened to Mog."

I stared at the big brown back of the truck, squinting as a picture of a box turtle seemed to emerge over the logo. And as I watched, his shell lifted and hovered just above his shoulders. If turtles have shoulders. The light changed. The truck turned. I twisted in my seat, staring after it before I said, "I think I know that."

Reilly pulled the car into the drive of the Hopkins House apartments and I started to get out, turning back at the last minute to ask, "After I left this morning, did Moma *say* anything? About where I was going, I mean?"

"She asked me to get carrot bread."

"Carrot bread?"

"As you were backing out of the driveway, I said I hoped it went well with the therapist you were going to see and that I thought it was a first-rate idea and about time, and Clara said, 'When you go to the store, would you pick up some carrot bread.' But try not to let your mother's reaction bother you too much, Annie, because you've got to know that as of today you've taken a giant step forward." She looked in her rearview mirror and said, "Uh-oh, there's a mail truck in back of me and I have to get going. Besides, I have to do Meals on Wheels. Have a good day and phone when you get off work so someone can pick you up."

I jumped out of the car, calling, "Thank you," and

watching as Reilly merged into traffic. I thought about what she called my giant step forward and about Moma and the stupid carrot bread—and the carrot bread won. In spite of myself, I felt my emotional high start to fizzle as I walked into the building.

By twelve-thirty it was just about all gone. By then, too, I'd eaten my lunch, swept the pool deck, checked the paper towel supply in the bathrooms, straightened rows of chaises that didn't need straightening, and tested the chlorine level of the water twice. And I was bored.

I'd been working at the pool at the Hopkins House since Monday, and so far it was hardly a whirlwind of activity. There's no snack bar, no soda machine, no baby pool, so it's pretty much for people who want to swim or grab a few rays. This particular day it was cool and a little bit cloudy, so the only people there were a man asleep on a chaise with *The Wall Street Journal* spread out over his face and a woman in a shower cap drifting in circles through the water. I watched her for a few minutes, then felt my eyes start to glaze over, the way they do when I watch fish swimming in a tank. I shook my head and pinched my arms and doodled on the bottom of the sign-in sheet. I went to the water cooler for a drink, then back to scoop leaves out of the pool with a skimmer. A fire engine raced by on University Parkway, and I stood at the wall and watched it snake its way through traffic.

When I turned around again, the shower-cap woman was standing on the cement and shaking herself like a big wet dog. After a few minutes I went back to the lifeguard's table, settling into my chair and watching the water turn smooth and flat.

"Wimp pool," Mog would have called it. "Fishpond, teacup, puddle." I closed my eyes and could hear her voice, teasing, laughing. "Give me the ocean any day. Give me tides and breakers and even an undertow. There's got to be a challenge, Annie."

I thought back to all the years we'd gone to the beach for our vacation and remembered Mog racing into the surf, calling, "Dare, dare," just before she dove under a wave. I remembered her catching rides on a boogie board and swimming beyond the breakers, waving back to me, urging me out. I remembered that Mog was never afraid.

Suddenly I felt cold and clammy and I got up to find my sweatshirt, pulling it on. "Mog was never afraid." I said the words out loud. My teeth chattered, and I was shaking on the inside as I thought about that last night. What had it been like for Mog? Had she been afraid then? Had the fear come after her, stalking her, or—

The shower-cap woman went by on her way out and said something about the weather. The *Wall Street Journal* man wasn't far behind, stopping at the table and offering me his paper. I nodded and mumbled something, and when he had gone I looked down to see that I'd twisted it to tatters.

Had Mog been afraid that night? The question nagged at me. When she and Bobby got back to the car and saw someone breaking in, had she known what was going to happen? Had she seen his face? Heard his voice? And what about the gun? What had she felt when she saw the gun?

But Mog was never afraid.

She ran at him, Bobby had told the policeman. To stop him, to chase him away. Had she called out, "Dare," I wondered. *Dare, dare.* Had she heard the shot? Known that it was meant for her? Or had it all happened too fast? And what about pain? Had she lived long enough to know that Bobby was there with her?

Had Mog been afraid?

She was never afraid.

But I was.

I was colder than I'd been before and I grabbed a beach towel and wrapped it around myself, leaning back in my chair and looking up at the balconies of the apartment house rising on the far side of the pool. I watched an orange cat move from one balcony to the next and wondered, idly, how he would find his way home again.

I remembered how, that morning, Harriet Jeffers had asked me if I knew why I was frightened, and when I couldn't tell her she'd said maybe we could get back to it. I wanted to get back to it this minute. I wanted to call and tell the answering service it was an emergency, and yank her away from whichever patient she was seeing. I wanted to tell her I was scared because the world wasn't a very safe place to be. I wanted to tell her I was scared because maybe it was my fault: maybe if I'd *insisted* on getting a ride with her and Bobby, and coming home with them, they wouldn't have gone off to Fells Point after the party. Wouldn't have surprised someone with a gun breaking into their car.

"Excuse me, but are you all right?"

I looked up to see a woman with two little girls standing next to the table, and I could tell from her face that she had been trying to get my attention for a while. "I'm sorry," I said. "I must've been spacing out."

"Must have been," she said. "I hope you don't do that

when there are people in the pool. Anyway, do you need to see my membership card?"

After I'd checked her card and had her sign in, she headed for the chaises, calling back over her shoulder, "Who'd have thought, this morning, that today would turn out like this?"

Then I realized that the sun was shining and the sweat was dripping down my back. I threw away my towel and peeled off my sweatshirt and took a running dive into the pool, swimming three quick laps before going back to my place.

"Fraternizing with the lifeguard allowed?" I looked up late in the afternoon to see Bobby Ritter standing at the table, holding his guest pass out to me.

"Bobby, hi," I said. "I didn't expect to see you here."

"I told you I'd come. So you'd know somebody, and from the looks of this place you could use a friend. Has it been like this all day?"

"Pretty much. Well, this morning the weather was yucky, but then this afternoon a few people drifted in, including a witch woman and her two little girls. She caught me spacing out when she got here and said she hoped I didn't do it when I was supposed to be lifeguarding, and then all afternoon I could see her watching me and waiting for me to drift off or something. And the thing is, I was concentrating so hard on her kids that I had to call them down twice for doing cannonballs onto a woman swimming laps. And the mother didn't like that *either*. But, as you can see," I said, pointing to the sign-in sheet, "it's not exactly Coney Island around here."

"It picks up on weekends, I think," said Bobby, heading for the dressing room to change.

When he came back he dropped his keys, watch, and wallet on the table, and as he turned toward the pool the scars on his arm seemed to flash hard and shiny. I must have gasped because he swung around. "Ahh," he said, "admiring my embroidery, huh?"

"It's—they're so real," I stammered.

"They're real, all right," he said as he continued to the pool.

"They're real, Annie," he said when he came back from swimming his laps and stood rubbing himself with a towel, pulling on a Virginia Tech sweatshirt. He sat down next to me and said, "The surgeon tried to tell me they'd fade, but I knew that even if they did they wouldn't. Not the real ones, anyway." He put his watch back on and sat looking at it for a minute. "In the beginning I thought that I should be dead, too. That it wasn't fair for me to be alive and Mog to—I thought about evening the score— what I thought would be evening the score."

"You don't mean—you wouldn't have—" I put my hand on his arm, but he shook me away.

"I wanted to die. Thought I should die. Just because some animal missed me and got Mog, why should I get to hang around for the next sixty years or so."

"Did the doctor talk you out of it? The one you were seeing?"

" 'Talk you out of it' is kind of simplifying it, but he worked at it. And my folks. And Father Nichols. I got everything from God's will to a lucky crapshoot. But I couldn't go with either of them. If God willed me to live, that same God sure as hell didn't will Mog to die. And I can't quite go with the crapshoot philosophy of life. So maybe, as Father Nichols said, it all has to do with a deeper purpose. Anyway, I did a lot of thinking. Still do, I guess. And those sixty years or whatever seem like a kind of trust now."

I nodded and we sat without saying anything until a mother and father and a couple of kids came in. "You lifeguard," said Bobby, "and I'll go down to the deli in the basement and get us some supper."

He came back with turkey sandwiches and cans of Coke, and we sat watching the kids dog-paddle across the pool and talked about learning to swim and who'd taught us and what it was like the first time we went off a high diving board. I told Bobby about my appointment with Harriet Jeffers and how I'd come out feeling almost floaty, which hadn't lasted but while it did was better than anything I'd felt in a long, long time.

"Yeah, it's a kind of euphoria," Bobby said. "It's like that sometimes. And then there'll be days when you come out angry and want to fight her with everything you've got."

When we had finished eating, Bobby went to get dressed. I sat watching the kids in the pool, waiting for their parents to call them out so I could begin to close up for the night. Once they had gone, I put the chaises into rows, picked up the trash, and locked the radio away in the closet. I was standing by the pool when Bobby came back.

"Ready?" he said.

"I've got to wait till eight," I said, checking my watch. "It's just a few more minutes." And then, maybe because even the traffic out on the street seemed suddenly quiet, I turned to him and said, "What was Mog like that last night, Bobby?"

"Great," he said. "The way she always was. We had a terrific time at the party, but we left a little early because Mog said we had to talk. That's why we went down to Fells Point in the first place. But once we got there it was so beautiful—the night and the moon and the water—we just walked and talked about graduation and college and the beginnings of things. And then, later, when I asked her what it was she'd wanted to say, she just said, 'Not now.' That we'd get to it another day. That there was plenty of time.

"Except there wasn't."

Relief washed over me. I was suddenly glad that Mog hadn't told Bobby what she'd set out to tell him that night, that there was no chemistry between them, no spark.

"Do you know what she wanted to talk about, Annie?" he said, catching me by the elbow.

I shook my head, turning away to pick up my towel. "Get real, Bobby. Mog and I were close, but she didn't tell me *everything*. Let's go."

When we got to the house, Moma and Dad were watching the news on CNN and Reilly was poring over her Elderhostel catalogue. "I think I've found something, Annie," she said after they'd greeted Bobby and asked if we'd had anything to eat and Moma had said there was half of a strawberry pie in the refrigerator. "Cooking for Two, how's that sound?"

"Great," I said. "Except that you hate to cook, Reilly,

and even if you took it up there are a lot more than two of us here."

"I know," she said. "I thought of that. But it's in Charleston, and I love Charleston. And besides, this place has private bathrooms."

I looked at Bobby and raised my eyebrows. "Reilly chooses her Elderhostel courses by the plumbing facilities."

"You're darn right," she said. "None of this down-the-hall business for me. Anyway, where would I hang my laundry?"

Moma laughed and got up and went into the kitchen, coming back a few minutes later with plates, forks, and the rest of the pie. We sat for a while, eating and talking and watching the news until Homer scrounged around under a table and came up with a tennis ball, carrying it over and dropping it at Bobby's feet.

"Okay, old buddy," Bobby said, getting up. "Can you play ball in the dark?"

"That dog could play ball in the dark *and* blindfolded," Dad called as we headed for the yard.

Later that night, as I was getting ready for bed, Moma stopped by my room, leaning in the open door to say, "He seems like a nice young man, Annie." As if she'd never seen Bobby Ritter before.

Eleven

"You're doing homework in summer? Even after you graduated?" Cricket said, coming along the side of the porch, climbing the railing, and somehow landing stretched out on the swing with his feet over one armrest and his head, at a weird angle, on the other.

"Here, take this, it might help," I said, tossing him a canvas pillow. "Besides, it's not homework."

"The great American novel, then?"

"Not that either. It's this thing I'm writing for Harriet that's supposed—"

"Who's Harriet?"

"Harriet Jeffers. The woman I've started seeing to help me straighten out the inside of my head."

"About Mog?" said Cricket.

"About Mog."

"Yeah, Dad told me you were gonna see somebody. And she makes you do *homework*?"

"It's not homework, I told you. Not the school kind, anyway. It's just that Harriet asked me to write this thing about where I want to be six months from now."

"Where do you?" Cricket asked, reaching down with one hand and pushing on the floor so that the swing lurched backward, and sort of sideways.

"Want to be? That's the funny part. Up till now I didn't have a clue, or even care. Only once I started to write it down, and the more I do, I think in six months' time where I want to be is college. Maybe, anyway."

"So go," said Cricket.

"It's not that easy. I mean, even if I were sure, which I'm not, it's almost the end of June, and assuming I could still get into any of the places that accepted me, it'd probably be too late for financial aid, and besides, I think there's a way you're supposed to do these things and sort of a time frame and—"

"So try," said Cricket.

"Then there'd be the whole question of where to go," I said, more to myself than to him. "Barnard is out. In fact it never really was in, and the only reason I applied there was that Ms. Hart sort of pushed me into it—because that's where Mog was going. That leaves either Loyola, here in town, or Mount St. Mary's, up in Emmitsburg, which I don't know anything about except that Ms. Hart said it was small and comfortable and she thought I'd like it, and besides, Erin's cousin went there and said they had great parties. But maybe I should go to Loyola. It's close to home and I could be a commuter and just slide into this whole thing gradually."

"Cripes, Annie, you've been doing that for twelve years. Go ahead and take the plunge," Cricket said, swinging around and shoving at the floor with his gigantic Nikes.

"But maybe I shouldn't," I said, as if he hadn't spoken. As if I hadn't heard Mog, somewhere in the back of my mind, calling, "Dare, dare."

"Shouldn't what?"

"Go to college. Not now, anyway. Maybe I should wait until things straighten out around here," I said, riffling the edges of the pages I'd written.

"What's to straighten out?" asked Cricket. "Reilly's normal, and Dad's okay, only sad, and Moma's weird. But she's only weird about Mog, and Coach Mac says maybe she'll always be that way and we'll just have to get used to it."

"Who's Coach Mac and what's he know about our mother?" I said.

"You know, he's Coach Mac, from school. Lacrosse. And he knows what I told him."

"How come?"

"Because he asked. You know, how things were going and all. He's like that. Cool."

"Does Dad know? About your talking to Coach Mac, I mean?"

"Yeah. He asked, too. When you started seeing that lady—"

"Harriet."

"When you started seeing her, Dad asked if I wanted to see someone, too. And I told him about Coach Mac. Anyway, I've got to go. I'm starving."

Cricket got up and headed off in the direction of the kitchen, but in a minute he was back, leaning against the porch rail and looking suddenly big and gangly, as if he'd grown while I wasn't watching. But when he spoke, his voice was small and hesitant. "Hey, Annie, can I tell you something?"

"Sure, Cricket. What?"

"It's just that, well, sometimes when I think about Mog—I can't remember what she looked like."

I wanted to rant at him. I wanted to scream and tell him we *had* to remember, that that was the only way we had of holding on to her. I wanted to make him feel rotten, and guilty, and about three inches tall. I didn't, though. Instead I chewed on the end of my pen and looked at him and said, "Me neither, Cricket. Me neither."

"My brother Cricket says that somebody named Coach Mac says Moma might always be the way she is now and we might just have to get used to it." I was sitting in Harriet Jeffers's office, the Koosh ball flying back and forth between my hands.

"How do you feel about that?" Harriet asked.

"That it stinks."

"Stinks because Coach Mac said it or because it may be a fact?"

"Both. He shouldn't have said it 'cause it shouldn't have been there for him *to* say. And it shouldn't be true," I said.

"Should—shouldn't. Should—shouldn't." Harriet repeated the words, then jotted them down on a piece of paper, holding the clipboard out for me to see. "I'd like for you to watch those *should* statements, Annie. When you direct them at yourself, they tend to make you feel pressured. And when you direct them at *others,* you're apt to end up feeling let down. Maybe resentful."

"But she *should.* Moma *should.* Get better, I mean. And acknowledge that Moggie died. That she lived."

"It would be helpful, or beneficial. It would make for a

better situation at home and make you happier, and your father, and Reilly, and Cricket. It would do a lot for your mother's mental health. Do you see the difference, Annie?"

I nodded, still whispering "Should—shouldn't" inside my head, not quite willing to let them go.

"Will she?" I asked. "Get better?"

"I don't know," Harriet said. "It could be that Coach Mac is right—that you all will have to learn to live with it. Right now your mother's in denial, but maybe one day that will change, maybe she'll be willing to work with someone and learn to deal with what's happened."

"Cricket says that Moma's only weird about Mog. That the rest of her is normal."

"Do you agree with that?"

"Yeah, maybe."

"What are some things your mother does that seem normal to you?"

"Well, she works. She's the 'Party Person' and puts on these fantastic parties for kids, and now she's even branching out to do some for grownups, too. She's a great cook—the kind where just ordinary weekday food tastes special. She still reads a ton and goes to museums and once even thought about being a docent, but the training program was really intense, so she's put it off for a while. The only thing is, though, that sometimes it's as if she's just going through the motions. Anyway, last night, when I told her and Dad at dinner that I was thinking maybe I wanted to go to college, after all, maybe to Mount St. Mary's, she said for me to call the director of admissions and then we could drive up there on my day off sometime and look it over."

"You've been thinking about college, then," said Harriet, shifting her position and easing her muumuu away from her body so that for a minute she looked like a head on top of a tent.

"How are the shingles?" I asked.

"Better, I think. I'm actually getting to the point where I believe I'll wear real clothes again. College?"

"I'm thinking of it. Maybe. I guess because of that paper you asked me to write, about where I want to be six months from now. I mean, just writing it made me start thinking. Are you going to read it, by the way?"

"I will if you want," said Harriet, taking the pages I held out to her. "But it was mostly for you."

"And I've talked to a bunch of people—to Dad and Moma and Reilly, and Cricket, too, who told me to take the plunge. To Erin and this other friend, and even to Sister Leonard when I saw her in the library.

"And I talked to Mog, too."

I bit my lip and waited, but when Harriet didn't say anything I went on. "I still do that some. Well, I don't actually *talk* to her as in a conversation, but I tell her things, about what's going on or what I'm thinking. And then I imagine what she'd say back to me."

"Which was?"

"Oh, same as Cricket. To take the plunge."

"But who has to make the ultimate decision, Annie?" Harriet said.

"I do. I have. I'm going."

"And have you called the admissions director?"

"No," I said, shaking my head. "But I will, today. It's just that, well, we've talked about this before, how now it's as if I'm going out ahead of Mog. Going on without her."

"Can you stand still, Annie? Anywhere in life?"

"And be like Moma," I said.

We didn't say anything for a minute and I realized how totally quiet Harriet's office was, as if layers of cotton batting were stacked up around us. "You know something," I said after a while, "Cricket told me he sometimes has trouble remembering what Mog looked like, and the thing is I sort of know what he means. Because it happens to me, too."

Harriet nodded.

"And then other times I see her as clearly as if she were right there beside me, only always the way she was that last day. It's weird to think that when I get to be an old lady, Moggie will still be seventeen."

All of a sudden a big ball of sadness and anger rolled over me, flattening me down, so that for a moment it was almost as though I couldn't get up again, couldn't catch my breath. "I feel cheated," I said, pounding my fist against the arm of my chair. "Cheated because I'll never get to see Mog graduate from college, and from med school, or grad school, or any other wonderful place she was going to go. Or cheer for her when she wins the Nobel Prize. I'll never get to be in her wedding, or her in mine, the way we always planned when we were little. Or see her pregnant. Or have a brother-in-law. Or be Aunt Annie to the children she'll never have. My kids won't get to play with *her* kids.

"Then I get so mad at her for leaving me the way she did, for forcing me to deal with it all. And afterward I end up feeling bad for thinking that way in the first place. Does any of this make sense?"

"It makes perfect sense," Harriet said, leaning over carefully and picking up the Koosh ball from where I'd dropped it on the floor and tossing it back to me.

After that we talked mostly about feeling guilty and not feeling guilty, and a little bit about my job. Harriet gave me an appointment for the following week, and it wasn't until she had walked me to the door that I said, all in a rush, "Oh, you know, that other friend I mentioned, when I said I talked to Erin and someone else, well, that was Bobby Ritter, who was Moggie's boyfriend and who's come by the pool a couple of times after work to take me home."

"Do you think that's a good idea, Annie, for either of you?" Harriet asked.

It was three times, actually, that Bobby had come by during the week. Three times that we sat together at the lifeguard's table, ate deli sandwiches, and swam laps just before it was time to close the pool for the night. Three times that he took me home and came in to say hi to Moma and Dad and Reilly, played ball with Homer in the backyard, and talked lacrosse with Cricket.

And Harriet Jeffers asked me if I thought it was a good idea.

I didn't answer her, though. Instead I kept on going down the hall and through the waiting room and out into the heat and humidity. Harriet's words seemed to jiggle at me as I got into the car and flipped on the ignition, the air-conditioning, the radio. I pulled out of the parking lot, looking back over my shoulder, half expecting to see her running after me, calling, "Do you think that's a good idea, Annie, for either of you?"

"Of course it's a good idea," I answered out loud. *"We're* a good idea. Bobby and I. We're safe and comfortable and used to each other. We're relaxed and not all awkward and wondering what to say or how to say it, the way we would if we were *new*. And we can talk about Mog." I caught my breath and went on. "Who does Harriet Jeffers think she is, anyway? Telling me what to do. Asking a question like that." I fumed and fussed as I overtook one truck and then another on the Beltway, remembering how Bobby had told me I wouldn't always come out of my sessions with Harriet feeling good. How sometimes I'd want to fight her with everything I had.

I was still upset when I went into the house, stepping around an umbrella stand in the shape of an elephant's foot that Moma was filling with sheaves of dried grasses.

"Bobby called," said Moma, standing back to look at what she'd done. "He's at home and wants you to call him."

I picked up the portable phone off the counter and carried it out to the porch, flopping onto the swing as I punched in Bobby's number. "Hi," I said when he answered. "It's me."

"What's wrong, Annie?" Bobby asked. "Your voice sounds funny. Like you're upset or something."

"Oh, it's nothing," I said, partly because Moma had brought her elephant's foot out onto the porch and was trying it in first one corner and then another, and partly because I wasn't really sure I wanted to tell Bobby that Harriet had questioned whether my seeing him was really a great idea. "I'm just sort of in a rush to get to work and all."

"That's what I wanted to talk to you about. My boss switched my schedule and I go in late and have to work tonight, so I won't be able to come by the pool. But I was wondering if whoever picks you up could drop you off down at the store. That is, if you wouldn't be bored out of your mind hanging out at scenic Video Americain."

"No, it'd be great," I said. "Almost as good as being lost in a bookstore. But I'll walk over—it's still light when I close up at eight."

The day seemed to stretch endlessly, and there were a lot of times when I wanted to push a button and fast-forward the whole thing. I wanted to yell at the swimmers to swim faster and found myself racing along as I cleaned the tiles or swept the deck. I tried not to look at the clock for a whole hour, a half hour, maybe fifteen minutes. When a new tenant in the apartment house came down to check out the pool, I hurried through my spiel, pointing out the dressing rooms, the sun deck on the upper level, telling about the occasional parties on Friday nights. The quicker the day went, the sooner I'd see Bobby. And whenever Harriet's voice echoed in my head—"Do you think that's a good idea, Annie?"—I told her to put a lid on it, to get lost, to mind her own business.

And finally it was eight o'clock. I glared at a man and his kids floating around the deep end on their backs like a bunch of sea otters, and took down the umbrella over the lifeguard's table, locking away the radio and lowering the wooden panels on the cabana. I picked up my towel and went to stand by the edge of the pool, pointing to the clock and calling, "It's time to close now." I watched as they took their own sweet time swimming to the side and climbing out and drying off and struggling, after what seemed like ages, into their shoes. As soon as they were gone, I dashed off to the dressing room and changed my clothes and was out of there.

Bobby was busy when I got to the store, so I wandered around, listening to the conversations between people trying to select a movie, running my fingers along the shelves, picking up old favorites and reading the blurbs on the boxes. Video Americain was a small, funky sort of place where you would never find a thousand and one copies of the latest hit but you *would* find all the offbeat movies you'd heard about and always wanted to see.

When the crowd thinned, I went behind the counter and sat with Bobby and he showed me where the movies that went with the empty video boxes were kept, and how to check them out. And later, when someone asked me for a really fabulous film I recommended my all-time favorite, *A Sunday in the Country,* even though Mog had always said it was boring and that nothing ever *happened*.

The store was busy until it closed at eleven, when Bobby and I went back to my house and sat side by side on the porch swing, talking some and listening to the sound of crickets, and feeling the current that seemed to pulse between us.

And when I went back to Harriet the next week, she didn't mention Bobby Ritter. And neither did I.

Twelve

The admissions director said okay. Well, she didn't exactly say "Okay" just like that, but after she finished with all the jargon and what Moma called "educationese," it came down to this: since I'd already been accepted and there was still room in the freshman class, they'd be glad to have me. And when she said, "Welcome to Mount St. Mary's," I got cold prickles all over me and half expected to see a red carpet unrolling right to the tips of my toes.

I'd felt that way since Moma and I had driven through Emmitsburg and turned off onto the road that led to the college. I'd felt that I *belonged* there. That it was a perfect summer's day didn't hurt any, and then there were the gently rolling hills that looked so close I was sure I could reach out and touch them, and yet seemed to go on forever. Before the official tour, we got out of the car and walked around a little on our own, looking up at the older gray stone buildings and the newer boxlike ones. We walked across parking lots and along paths, making our way over to the chapel, which seemed to draw us.

Not that I was super-religious or anything. Not that I

was planning on spending a whole lot of time *in* the chapel. But still, it seemed significant that it was there and sort of in the middle of things. Moma pushed the door open and we went inside, walking down a side aisle and back up the center, squinting at the Stations of the Cross niched into the walls and breathing the warm waxy smell. We slid into the last pew and sat for a few minutes, not saying anything.

All of a sudden I had the overwhelming feeling that Mog was there with me. I looked over at Moma to see if she sensed it, and she was staring straight ahead.

"I wish Moggie was here," I said, my voice sounding louder than I had meant it to. "I wish she could see it all with us."

I half held my breath, afraid of how Moma would react.

"I do, too," I thought I heard my mother say. "I do, too," I heard again.

But when I turned to her, she was pointing to her watch and nodding toward the door, and we got up and went outside without saying more, blinking at the rush of sunlight all around us.

"Now for the interview," I said, feeling nervous for the first time and dragging my feet a little as we made our way back to the main building. "What if they don't like me? What if they think I'm nothing but a wimp who couldn't make up her mind and I don't *deserve* to come to college? What if they want somebody with better grades or higher SATs?"

"Your grades were great, and so were your SATs," said Moma in typical mother fashion. "Just think of what your father told you."

"Yeah, right, I'll pull it out of that grab bag of good wishes they all sent me off with this morning. 'Wow 'em' from Dad. 'To keep from being nervous, just think of the interviewer sitting there in her underwear' from Reilly. And 'Chill out' from Cricket. Do you have anything to contribute?"

"Be yourself," said Moma, and I groaned as we went up the steps and opened the door.

The admissions director was younger than I thought an admissions director would be. She wore a red suit with a short skirt and her hair was cut in a kind of cap close to her head, in a way that looks great if you can wear your hair that way. Which she could. And if I imagined *her* in her underwear it'd have to be something tiny and filmy and straight out of Victoria's Secret.

"Hi, Annie, Mrs. Fitzhugh," she said. "My name is Liza Goode, and I want to get to know you and have you get to know us. But I was thinking, since it's such an absolutely perfect day, why don't we wander through the campus and we can talk as we walk. Okay?"

"Fine," I said, feeling suddenly relieved and reasonably sure that a stroll through the campus on a summer's day couldn't be as traumatic as sitting across a mile-wide desk while some glinty-eyed admissions director hurled questions at me. Like the one who asked Mog to define *relative* in fifty words or less—and he didn't mean her brother or grandmother or aunt either. I was just starting to relax when Moma pulled a paperback out of her purse and said, "I'll leave you to get to know each other, and I'll meet you at the bench out front when you're done." And before I could even give her a don't-abandon-me look, she was gone.

"Relax, Annie," said Liza Goode. "There's only one requirement from these interviews, here anyway. That you—"

"Be yourself," we both said, and laughed.

In the beginning we talked mostly about high school and what I'd done there and what I was doing this summer. Then Liza (that's how I thought of her, though I didn't actually *call* her anything) asked me what had appealed to me about Mount St. Mary's.

"Because Megan Hart, our guidance counselor at St. Kit's—St. Christopher's—said it was comfortable," I said.

"Comfortable? Yes, I guess we are comfortable up here," Liza said. "But never complacent. We like to think of ourselves as being on the cutting edge. Our students do *well*. And those who apply to grad schools are accepted by some of the best."

We visited the administration offices, which were basic boring, then moved on to look at labs and classrooms and from there to one of the dorms, where the word of choice definitely would have to be *barren*. I guess Liza knew what I was thinking, because she suddenly went into a spiel about how, by the end of the first day of school, I'd hardly recognize this place. I stood at the door of one of the rooms looking at two beds, two desks, two chairs, two dressers, and listened to her go on about plants and posters and pictures from home, and gradually a room straight out of *Seventeen* began to emerge. "And," said Liza, finishing up with a flourish, "sometime soon you'll want to get in touch with your roommate so you can decide who's to bring what—as far as curtains and bedspreads and maybe even a small refrigerator go."

From the dorm we went on to the library, where we wandered through the first floor and talked about books. Liza asked me what I was reading now and what was the best book I'd ever read, and I said, *Gone With the Wind,* then felt really dumb and had to explain. "That's what I'm reading now because I'd never actually *read* it, only seen the movie, and at the pool I have to read something like that. Something where it doesn't matter if I start and stop and start again.

"But the best book I ever read—the very best—was actually three books called *Kristin Lavransdatter,* which Reilly bought me one day at a used-book sale and I started during the flu last year and just kept reading. They're all about the Middle Ages and so intense that sometimes, when people would interrupt me, I'd have trouble getting back to the real world. If you know what I mean."

After we had seen the library we went outside and sat on a stone wall, and Liza asked me if I knew what I wanted to major in, what I wanted to *do* after college.

"Mostly I know what I *don't* want to do," I said.

"Which is?"

"Anything to do with math or medicine or very little children. But I don't know what I want *to* do, at least not the way my friend Erin wants to be a lawyer and my brother, Cricket, who's only fourteen, has his whole career as a sports announcer mapped out. That's the problem. You're *supposed* to know."

"Not necessarily, Annie. That's one of the things college helps you with."

Then, maybe because the sun was warm on my back

and I felt safe and comfortable, I heard myself saying things I'd said only once before, and that time to Mog. "I pretty much know that I want to be behind things."

"Behind things?"

"Behind the scenes. I read this article once about a young woman who was in charge of all the details when the Baltimore Symphony went to Asia. You know, like travel arrangements and hotels and how the instruments were packed so nothing happened to them. Well, that's the kind of thing I want to do.

"I mean, I don't want to *write* a book, but I might like to help somebody else's manuscript turn *into* a book. I'm not an actress, but I might like to do something with the theater, or maybe even be in charge the *next* time the symphony goes to Asia, or anywhere else for that matter."

Then I stopped, wanting to grab my words back, sure somehow that Liza Goode was giving me black marks on her mental scorecard. Sure that admissions directors were programmed to approve only of applicants who wanted to *play* in the symphony, *write* the bestsellers, *star* in the shows.

Instead she said it sounded as though I had a pretty good idea of what I wanted to do, in spite of myself. And how behind the scenes very often was where the action was. Then she got up and led the way down toward the gym, which still seemed to smell of sweat socks even though it was summer vacation. As we headed back and started up the hill to where Moma was waiting, Liza said, "You mentioned a brother, Cricket, I think. Are there any other children in your family, Annie?"

I stood for a minute without saying anything. I saw Moma get up, saw her start toward us. "Well, how was it?" she called.

I turned back to Liza, shook my head quickly, and said, "No, just Cricket and me."

"I didn't tell her about Mog. It was as if I *denied* her, pretended that she'd never existed. And all because Moma was there and coming toward us, and I didn't want to take a chance on Moma's freaking out or else getting all cold and stony the way she sometimes does."

"Come on, Annie," said Bobby, "give yourself a break. Just because you don't tell some college admissions director you don't even know about your sister doesn't mean you denied her, for gosh sakes. It was expediency, pure and simple. Besides, you don't always have to tell everybody *everything*."

"I hope you're right."

"Trust me."

Bobby and I were at Oregon Ridge, a park and onetime ski slope out in the county, where the Baltimore Symphony sometimes plays in summer. We were sitting on a blanket with the remains of our picnic supper spread out around us, waiting for the intermission to be over and the Viennese Night concert to resume, having the same conversation for the second, maybe the third, time. But somehow I couldn't let go of it, couldn't get over the feeling that I'd turned away from Mog.

The musicians came onto the stage and took their places and I settled back, leaning on my elbows and looking at the stars overhead. After they tuned up, the orchestra launched into *Tales from the Vienna Woods,* and I swayed in time to the music, remembering how Reilly used to play that same piece on the piano as Mog and I, draped in a pair of discarded yellow curtains, swirled and swooped through the whole downstairs. How we arrived back at the piano in time to take our bows, just after the final chord. And always begged for more.

The music went on, catching me up, carrying me along so that I wasn't always sure whether the time was now or then, whether I was lying on a blanket at Oregon Ridge or collapsing in a heap with Mog, calling, "Encore, encore."

When the concert was over, Bobby and I gathered up our blanket and cooler and made our way along the path to the parking lot. The way was dark and the ground bumpy underfoot, and as I turned to say something I stumbled and fell into him. He caught hold of me, dropping the cooler and wrapping his arms around me, steadying me. And suddenly, somehow, we were clinging to each other, breathing each other in. The crowd surged behind us and someone coughed. Someone else called, "Move along up there."

We broke apart and made our way to the car, fumbling for the locks, almost falling inside, moving close. Bobby's lips tasted salty, and I thought of oceans and pretzels and tears. It became bright around us, and I opened my eyes to see headlights coming on and the parking attendant swinging his flashlight as our row of cars started to move. I pulled back and Bobby flipped on the ignition, touching me lightly on the chin as he turned onto the road.

Neither of us spoke on the way home. A late night jazz show was playing on the radio and Bobby kept time against the steering wheel, whistling raggedly. And I, feeling shaken and disoriented, slid down low in my seat, thinking, No, no. You can't.

"No," I said as we pulled up in front of the house and Bobby switched off the car and reached for me. "No, Bobby, don't you see." I opened the door and got out and he followed me, coming to stand beside me.

"I don't understand," he said. "It seemed so right, so good—back there when we . . ."

I shook my head and looked up at the streetlight. "Don't you see—it's too confusing right now. I mean, here I am trying to get my thinking straight about Mog and this—what happened—what's happening between us—it'll just muddy the waters. I mean, I like being with you—so much that I sometimes wish those nights at the pool could go on forever." I was babbling, but I couldn't seem to stop. "But can't you see it, Bobby? I'm not Mog. I can't *ever* be Mog for you."

I waited, desperate for Bobby to say that he knew I wasn't Mog. That he knew I was Annie. That he wanted me *because* I was Annie. I crossed my fingers and willed him to say all that.

He didn't, though.

After a while he shuffled his feet and said, his voice husky, "I guess you're right, Annie. I guess I just wanted things to be the way they used to be."

Thirteen

Harriet Jeffers didn't say, I told you so. She didn't say that she'd tried to warn me, or that I should have known better, or that Bobby and I ending up together would've been the stuff of storybooks.

We sat in her office the morning after the night at Oregon Ridge, the morning after I'd placed a frantic call to her answering service and waited, crouched over the phone, for her to call me back.

"It was like 'Sleeping Beauty' and 'Beauty and the Beast' and all the fairy tales I ever read lumped into one. It was all the frogs turned into princes and one gigantic 'happily ever after.' And there were no ogres until . . ."

"Until?" prompted Harriet.

But I shook my head and held up my hand. "It's just that these last few weeks have been so great, with Bobby and all."

Harriet held out a box of Kleenex and I wiped the tears I hadn't known were pouring down my face.

"It hurts, Annie, doesn't it?" Harriet said.

I nodded, not sure I could go on. But after a while I

said, "And it hurts for so many reasons. Because it was so right between Bobby and me I began to know that maybe I'd always been a little bit in love with him, even when he was Mog's boyfriend. And because last night, when he was holding me and I wanted it to go on forever, I knew, without knowing how I knew it, that it wasn't going to. And mostly it hurts because, more than anything, I wanted Bobby to want me for being Annie. And he couldn't."

"He was honest," said Harriet.

"Yeah." I snorted, reaching for another Kleenex. "He was honest. And the trouble is, none of it makes sense. I mean, *I* was the one who pulled away from *him*, who said that things were too complicated right now. So why should I feel jilted?"

"It happens, Annie. The heart leading one way and the head another," said Harriet.

We just sat there then, neither of us saying anything, and after a while it seemed that the way Harriet kept offering me tissues, a trash can for the used ones, and, later on, the Koosh ball, was as good as the magic spell I'd hoped she'd cast. Finally I let out a sigh that reached all the way to the bottoms of my feet and said, "I almost forgot—Moma and I went up to Mount St. Mary's yesterday."

"And how'd that go?" asked Harriet.

"I really liked it and they have room for me and want me to come and I told them I would and there's a roommate out there who's going to get in touch with me, or else I'll get in touch with her, as soon as I find out her name."

"How do you feel about all that, Annie?"

"Well," I said, "when I stop feeling bad I think I'll feel good."

By noon the temperature was ninety-eight and the pool was crowded. There were people there I'd never seen before, stretched out on chaises, huddled under the awning down by the deep end, sitting on the sides and dangling their legs, or drifting slowly through the water. Fathers went off to the deli and came back with children dripping ice cream sandwiches, and mothers served sodas and apple juice out of coolers. A man intent on swimming laps wove his way between boys playing Marco Polo and finally gave up, claiming a place along the side of the pool and starting in on his crossword puzzle instead. A woman sat cross-legged on a towel, spritzing herself with water from a plastic Windex bottle. And I felt more like a referee than a lifeguard, calling out, "No running," "No ball playing," "No swinging on the steps," until I was tired of listening to myself.

By five o'clock the place had thinned out and I went around picking up trash, gathering towels and flip-flops and paperback books that had been left behind, and storing them on the shelf next to the water cooler. I rearranged the chaises and called the maintenance man about the sink that was clogged up in the men's bathroom. The heat was still oppressive, and I dove in at the deep end and swam the length of the pool underwater, but no sooner had I climbed out than I began to sweat again, even before my suit had started to dry.

I knew that while the pool was empty and before the after-work crowd arrived, I should run down to the deli and get some supper. But I didn't. I thought about calling Erin to see if she wanted to do something that night, but I didn't do that either. I opened my copy of *Gone With the Wind* and tried to read, but I couldn't concentrate and shoved the book across the table. People started to drift in, and I looked up at each one eagerly, half expecting to see Bobby. I played games with the clock, telling myself if I didn't check it for five, ten, fifteen minutes he would be there. Except that I knew he wouldn't. And at eight o'clock I called Reilly for a ride home.

The heat wave stretched on into the next week, wilting people, wearing them down, and on days when the temperature topped one hundred the pool was largely deserted, as if everyone had decided to stay home, close to the air-conditioning. When there was no one in the water I moved over under the weeping willow tree at one end of the enclosure, lying down and looking through the branches at the hard blue sky. Other times I sat under the umbrella, slathering myself with sun block and reading *Gone With the Wind.*

On my days off I called Erin. If she was free, we'd go shopping for college clothes, except whenever we got to the mall we weren't sure what we wanted and ended up eating lunch in the food hall and heading off to the movies instead.

I got a letter from someone at Mount St. Mary's, saying that my roommate's name was Mary Helen Potter and that she lived in Springfield, Virginia. A few days later I got a letter from Mary Helen herself, only she signed it Minnie, adding, in parentheses, that her brother had thought she looked like a mouse when she was little and that the name had stuck. It was a careful letter, like the beginning of a conversation with a person you meet on a train for the first time, and was all about how her mother had bought bedspreads that weren't too bad and she'd bring those and her CD player along if I could come up with a little refrigerator and maybe a small microwave if we were allowed to have one. She said that she was working for a lawn care service this summer and was looking forward to college and should we get a phone. She asked me to write back, or maybe call, and said that we could meet in Washington one day except that she was going to the beach for the last week in August and that didn't leave much time, especially since she was still working and she presumed I was, too.

By the time she got to the P.S., Mary Helen/Minnie began to sound like a real person and not someone handing in an assignment to "write a letter to a friend" for freshman English class in high school. She talked about her dog, a Dalmatian named Spot ("Well, what do you expect from a family who name their kid after a mouse?"), her brothers (two older, one younger), her mother, who wrote children's books, and her father, who owned the lawn service company ("which goes a long way to explain why I work there"). She said she was small, but mighty, and that come to think of it, maybe she did look something like a mouse. She wanted to know what music I liked and if I was into progressive or alternative, and how I felt about Pearl Jam, Nirvana, and R.E.M. And did I care if she put her Grand Canyon poster on the outside of the closet door ("sort of a space for a space"), but not to sweat it, it could always go on the inside. The P.S. ended up being almost as long as the letter.

I wrote back and told Minnie about my lifeguard job and Homer the dog and Ben the cat and how I was looking forward to college, too. I said I already had a little refrigerator from the time Reilly broke her leg and had to stay upstairs and wanted a ready supply of Cokes at hand, and that Nana and Popoo were giving me the microwave as a going-off-to-college present and did we need curtains because we had an attic full of stuff and I was sure I'd be able to come up with something. I couldn't tell her about Mog and I couldn't *not* tell her, so I pretty much left out my family, except for Reilly, and probably ended up sounding like an only child, or maybe an orphan. I finished by saying that I'd see her in September and that her "space for a space" sounded intense and that I'd bring my poster of Monet's waterlilies, which I'd gotten at the museum this summer.

One night, when Moma picked me up after work, we came home to an empty house. Dad and Cricket were at an Orioles game, and Reilly had gone to Deep Creek Lake with a friend. I was rummaging in the fridge for something to eat when I heard Moma say, "I certainly do miss seeing Bobby around here, Annie." I stood for a minute, staring down at a package of turkey in my hand, watching the way the label curled against the paper and trying to think how to change the subject.

"Annie?" Moma said.

And I straightened up to face her, closing the refrigerator door and saying, "It wouldn't have worked, Moma. It couldn't have. It was a relationship that wasn't going anywhere."

"But he seemed like such a nice young man."

"But he was Moggie's nice young man, Moggie's boyfriend, don't you see that. And I'm not Mog, Moma, and I can't ever be. Not for Bobby or for anyone else."

My mother froze and moved away, but I went to stand in front of her, the words beating inside of me. "Why won't you talk to me about Mog?" I heard myself say. "Why won't you talk about her to Dad or Cricket or Reilly? Why won't you?"

My mother's face was smooth and white, like the face of a statue. Homer stirred in his sleep, and the kitchen was quiet except for the hum of the ceiling fan going round and round.

"I can't," she said after a while, and she turned and went up the back stairs.

Fourteen

The rest of the summer went by in a whirl, like the blur the Koosh ball made when I threw it up into the air. I went to work every day and came home again, and even finished *Gone With the Wind* and thought about starting *Scarlett* but didn't, deciding to save it for next summer, in case I worked as a lifeguard again. I watched a bunch of movies on the VCR with Cricket and got into the habit of going with Dad and Homer every night when they took their walk. Moma and I went shopping for a slicker, new jeans, and underwear, and enough Kleenex and tooth-paste and shampoo to last my whole four years of college. And Reilly and I rooted in the attic and found a pair of curtains we thought would be okay for my room in the dorm.

I kept on going to see Harriet Jeffers and we talked about Mog, the way we always did, only now my feelings weren't as raw and ragged as they'd been before. We also talked about Moma and what she'd said in the chapel at Mount St. Mary's and how her saying "I can't" when I asked why she wouldn't talk to me about Mog was at least an acknowledgment of my sister's death. And we talked about how the police had told Dad, the last time he asked, that they probably would never know who killed Mog— that it would go on being an open file.

"You'll have to work on a sense of closure, Annie," Harriet said.

"That's not the same as forgetting, is it?" I asked.

"Not the same at all."

The week before Labor Day a bunch of my friends who had been working down at the beach came home to get ready for college, and we all got together at Erin's house. We made quesadillas and swam in the pool and, when a storm came up, went into the house and watched the video Erin's dad had made of us right before graduation in the spring. And just *watching* it made us feel old and sort of removed and as if we'd already taken a step away from that earlier time.

On my last day off from work, Dad took Moma, Cricket, Reilly, and me to Camden Yards to see an Orioles game. It was during the fifth inning, when I'd gone out to the concession stand to get a Coke, that I ran into Bobby Ritter. He was balancing two hot dogs and two drinks and a bag of chips on one of those wobbly cardboard trays they give you, and trying to stuff his wallet back into his pocket at the same time. "Here, I'll hold that," I said, taking the tray.

Afterward we stood there for a while, looking over each other's shoulders and talking about the game and the weather and how we'd both be heading off to college soon.

"Well, I guess I'd better get this stuff back," Bobby

said, reaching out for the tray. "But see you, Annie. And have a great time in college." I watched him go up the ramp and disappear into the stadium and half wanted to run after him, to talk to him a little longer, to see whom he was with. And after I got back to my seat I twisted and turned, looking over my shoulder and up into the crowd, trying to find Bobby.

"Earth to Annie, earth to Annie. The game's that way," I heard Cricket say as he pointed to the field. "And the O's just got a run."

The pool closed on Labor Day, and the next day I started packing in earnest, running out to the store for empty boxes, shoving snow boots and sheets and blankets into plastic leaf bags, bumping an old army foot locker from the attic to the first-floor hall and filling it with clothes I'd carried from my room. I found an old bookcase nobody wanted and dragged it downstairs, laying it flat and filling the spaces with my plants, extra sweaters, my yellow sweatpants. I packed up my computer and stashed it next to the piano, balancing a laundry basket filled with towels on top. I ran up and down the steps, adding my clock radio, a stuffed tiger, and a slightly tattered rag rug to the mountain of things rising in the front hall.

"We'll have to take two cars," said Moma, working her way through to the steps. "And if you don't stop adding things we'll have to enlist Reilly and her car, too."

"Count me out," said Reilly. "You know I hate good-byes."

"Don't you want to see my school?" I asked.

"Tell you what," said Reilly. "The first time you want to come home for the weekend, I'll pick you up. I can see it then. Besides, I don't want to be around when your roommate sees all this stuff rolling in."

"All *this* stuff? Wait'll you see what *she's* bringing. Her family's rented a U-Haul. Anyway, this is absolutely *it,* except for the clothes that are in the dryer and my photo album and the jewelry box that's on my dresser, except I can't pack that until tomorrow. But there's a space saved—between the blue and green towels in the laundry basket."

Dad has a thing about scientific packing, and he spent ages the next morning studying the things in the front hall, mentally measuring and sorting and dividing up between his car and Moma's. Then he stood on the driveway, calling out "Trunk . . . bookcase . . . laundry basket . . . refrigerator . . . boxes . . . ," while Cricket and I raced back and forth to get them.

"There," he said, finally straightening up and wiping his hands down the sides of his khakis. "A place for everything and everything in its place. All it takes is planning. Better check inside, Annie, to see if we've forgotten anything. There's an unclaimed three inches in the back of my car."

I went across the front lawn and into the house, catching my breath at the way the normally cluttered hall seemed suddenly spare. I ran my fingers along the top of the pie safe and banged on one of the drums. I stood for a minute next to the player piano, before wandering into the living room, flopping down onto the couch, looking up at cousin George's model airplanes moving in the breeze from the open window. I swallowed hard at the rush of homesickness that washed over me and got up to stand in front of the Mizpah Picture, putting my finger on the

Mog girl, the Annie girl, thinking how this time I really was going on without Mog. But how, in a way, she'd always be with me. "The Lord Watch between Me and Thee . . ." I whispered as I picked up my backpack and went outside.

I rode with Dad, and Cricket rode with Moma, and we met at an inn in Reisterstown for lunch. Cricket and Dad joked about its being my last meal before the college dining hall, and Moma said they'd send CARE packages. The trouble was that though I was hungry I couldn't eat. There were giant butterflies in my stomach and a lump in my throat the size of a basketball. I wanted to hurry up and get there—and I wanted to turn around and go home. I wanted Dad and Moma to slow down just long enough to drop me off—and I wanted to hang on to them, to never let them go. I wanted to be in college—and I wanted to stay in high school forever.

The parking lots at the college were swarming with cars and vans and U-Hauls. There were people carrying bags and boxes, suitcases and trunks. A man balanced a floor lamp across his shoulders, and two girls went by holding a rocking chair between them. There were signs with arrows pointing to the dorms and upper-class students answering questions. Dad found a space close to my dorm, and Moma pulled in beside us. We parked and got out, stepping into air that seemed electrically charged.

"Come on!" I called. "Let's hurry."

"Don't go empty-handed," Dad said as he unlocked the trunk and handed me the laundry basket, perching the stuffed tiger on top.

When we got to my room, there was a note taped onto the door. "Welcome, Annie, from Minnie. Don't faint when you see the room—*it will all fit*. I promise you. Meanwhile we've gone to get something to eat. Be right back. XXX."

And it's a good thing she warned me. We opened the door and let out a gasp, staring at the trunk, the boxes, the laundry basket, all clones of what I'd brought. "Well," said Moma, shoving a duffel bag out of the way with her foot, "you could always use the room as a closet and sleep in the hall."

Dad and Cricket crowded in behind us, groaning as they lowered the foot locker onto an empty space over by the radiator. We headed down to the car for another load, and another and another, leaving Moma upstairs to try to clear a place in the middle of the floor. When we got back with the last of the bags and a basket of coat hangers, Minnie and her parents were there, wedged in with Moma, and the rest of us piled in on top. We introduced ourselves, and the room echoed with bits of conversations. Dad and Mr. Potter moved out into the hall to talk baseball and Cricket went off and reappeared a few minutes later with a can of Coke, announcing that the vending machines were on the first floor around the corner from the water fountains. Moma dug a pair of sheets out of a leaf bag, which must have been a motherly thing to do because Mrs. Potter was already making Minnie's bed.

"Well, what do you think?" said Minnie, pulling her hair back and twisting it into a bun.

"I think it's great, going to *be* great," I said.

"You're right. Great." She dug in her backpack for the Scotch tape, unrolled her Grand Canyon poster, and fastened it carefully to her closet door. "I can't wait to get settled."

"Me neither," I said. I found my laundry basket behind the desk and rooted down among the towels for my jewelry box and the picture that had been taken two years ago last Easter, putting it on the corner of my dresser.

"Is that your family?" said Minnie, coming to stand beside me. "Is that your grandmother?" she said, pointing to Reilly.

"That's Reilly. My cousin, or my father's cousin once removed, or something. She's cool."

"And this is . . . ?" Her finger tapped the glass under Mog.

"That's Mog, my sister."

"Oh, is she at Mount St. Mary's, too? Or some other college?"

There was a sudden silence in the room. Moma straightened up, leaving the bed half made, dropping the pillow, the pillowcase. She came over to me, catching my face between her hands. "It's okay, Annie. Tell her about Mog." Then she kissed me on the forehead and left the room.

"Did I say something wrong?" asked Minnie.

"No, it's okay," I said. "It's just that Moggie was killed not long after this picture was taken. I'll tell you about it sometime."

Mr. Potter and Dad were in the doorway, talking about heading home, beating the traffic on the Beltway. "Anyway, the sooner you get this stuff unpacked, the better off you'll be," said Minnie's mother, putting the case on my pillow, smoothing the top sheet.

We all stood for a minute as if we weren't sure what

was supposed to happen next, until Minnie caught her mother by the arm and called to her father, "Okay, you guys, out into the hall for the big Potter family goodbye scene."

Dad put his hands on my shoulders and pulled me close. "Good luck, Annie, and don't worry about your mother. It'll work out, I'm sure of it."

Cricket slapped me five, then pulled out of the way when he thought I was going to kiss him.

"Don't come down," Dad said as I followed them to the door, and I hugged him quickly, then stood with my eyes closed, listening to their footsteps going along the hall. When I couldn't hear them anymore I ran to the window, hanging out and waiting for my father and brother to appear down below.

"Well, this is it," said Minnie, her voice sounding small and choked as she came to stand beside me.

"Yes," I said, swallowing hard. "This is it."

We stood together watching as the Potters and Dad and Cricket made their way across the parking lot, looking back, calling up to us. I saw my mother standing beside her car, saw her bend down to unlock the door, then saw her straighten up and turn slowly. I saw her wave.

" 'Bye, Moma," I yelled, even though I was sure she couldn't hear me. " 'Bye, Moma."

"Okay," said Minnie when they had all gone, "shall we unpack or check out the campus?"

"Unpack, *then* check out the campus," I said. "Besides, there's a dorm meeting in an hour and a half. That'll give us plenty of time to settle in." And I turned to the bookcase, taking out the plants and lining them along the windowsill, dropping my yellow sweatpants and the extra sweaters into the bottom drawer of one of the dressers. I righted the bookcase and pushed it over against the wall and stood back. "There," I said, "the place looks better already. Don't you think?"